The Warder

Susie Williamson

Stairwell Books //

Published by Stairwell Books
161 Lowther Street
York, YO31 7LZ

www.stairwellbooks.co.uk
@stairwellbooks

Paperback ISBN: 978-1-913432-19-5
eBook ISBN: 978-1-913432-20-1

Layout and cover design: Alan Gillott
Cover Images by Wangkun Jia, rck_953 and Valentyna
Chukhlyebova

1. Luna

I HAD NO MEMORY OF getting to the mountains, yet I found myself standing on the flat-topped summit. A distant screech pierced the skies. I looked up and saw the dragon of my nightmares flying like an arrow towards me.

Was I dreaming? I had never dreamt of the mountains before. My dreams were of the forest, keeping to the cover of trees as the dragon searched from above the canopy. I should have run but here, out in the open, there was nowhere to hide. I felt my heart thumping in my chest as I stepped back.

That was the moment I broke, the moment I realised I had stepped outside my own body.

Bewildered, I looked at my ten-year-old self: I held up my hands, tried to pat my arms, but I had no more form than a ghost. I parted my lips and mouthed the word, *how*, but the silent part of me had no sound. I moved in front of the girl for a closer look. There was terror on her face, her hands were clenched into fists, as she stood frozen staring up at the sky.

The girl gripped the shawl tight around her shoulders as the dragon descended, its beating wings stirring a cold wind. I stepped to the side, standing next to the girl, watching the dragon's awkward landing, the ground trembling beneath the weight of its massive bulk. Its flight appeared effortless, but on land it stumbled. Its leathery wings, webbed like a bat's, stepped forward in turn, the clawed digit at the end of each bony forearm stabbing the ground. The barbed tail swung from side to side as it dragged behind. Its long neck swept low to the ground, reaching its angular, grey head towards the girl. We looked into the cold stare of its silvery blue eyes, and saw the vertical slit pupils widen into circles. Gazing into these dark pools they appeared to come alive, swirling like liquid, slowly forming a distant image. As the image became clearer for both parts of us to see, I realised that it was a scaled down version of my reflection.

Wisps of smoke from the dragon's flared nostrils reeked like charred meat, as it breathed, as though smelling the girl. Then it swung its neck to the side and up, lifting its head high and back as it opened its jaws, exposing yellowed fangs. The screeching roar came first, followed by its fiery breath streaming down. Surrounded by flames, I heard the girl's screams and watched her writhe in pain. I grabbed her arms, wanting to drag her away. For a brief moment her skin was all I could feel, then came the searing heat of the fire and the realisation I was back in my own body, holding up my arm in a futile attempt to shield my face.

Something grabbed my shoulders from behind and swung me round. Still burning, I kicked and screamed, trying to pull away from the man I called my father.

'Dragon fire!' I yelled, as he picked me up and held me close. I pummelled my fists against his chest, but he just looked at me bewildered.

My face was still burning but I saw no fire. I turned to see the dragon was gone.

2.   Wanda

I RETURNED TO THE CAVE with an armful of kindling, dropped it on the meagre woodpile, and knelt down, striking the flint. Once the fire was smoking and a pot of water was on to boil, I reached up to pluck mint leaves from the dried bouquet hanging from the roof. I stopped, feeling cold brush against the back of my neck, and dropped my arm back down by my side. Air filled my lungs but I couldn't breathe. I was unbound but I couldn't move, gripped by the cold seeping into me. It lasted just a moment, but that moment seemed to stretch with each passing day, month and year. I offered a fleeting glance at the thing that haunted me: the shadow, my curse.

The cave was my retreat from the world, but I could never truly be alone. The wretched shadow was always close, like a predator stalking its prey. The ghostly man-shaped form usually appeared in shifting tones of grey, but sometimes, like now, it darkened to black when it sang its haunting tune. Clicking, humming and screeching like swarming insects rose out of the shadow, echoing around the cave. As the notes came together, rising and falling in waves, it was as though the shadow was tempting me, willing me to look into its dark depths. The harmony of notes slowly blended to form the slow drawling word, '*Oraaag*'. Today it sounded like a long low growl. Other times I heard its pitch like a sweet song floating in the breeze, but there was nothing sweet or innocent about the spirit of Orag. I turned away and walked out of the cave. Sitting with legs dangling over the overhanging shelf, I looked out over the grasslands, ignoring the shadow's song.

3

I was eighteen years old or thereabouts, but ten long years bound to the shadow left me feeling aged and tired. Living in the valley, surrounded by nature, I wondered if it was the surrounding boundless life that kept the shadow from consuming me entirely. Wildlife had always been my sanctuary. I was still known as the boy with a gift, but no one knew how far I had strayed, or the shadow I had unleashed all those years ago. They only knew how my gift had brought me face to face with our Great Spirit, the Mantra. It was an encounter that saw balance return to my homeland, but afterwards, at eight years old, I was not the same boy.

The voice of Orag had started speaking to me, plaguing me night and day. It was the Mantra's equal and opposite, an evil spirit that had once attacked my homeland. Now it was back, taunting me, calling me, beckoning me to the mountains. Finally, I followed it into the high slopes, where a man-shaped shadow rose up out of the cold barren rock. When its black wispy fingers reached out and touched my skin, the feeling of cold death settled in my stomach. I fled, but the shadow's song stayed close at my heels. There was nowhere to hide from the creature that was bonded as tightly as my own skin.

All these years later, I couldn't tell where I ended and the shadow began. I was haunted by the thought that I was evil. After all, why else would an unworldly spirit have attached itself to me?

I watched a herd of grazing red deer move slowly east. The sun was shining but the colours of the grasslands were muted, distorted by the shadow's bond. It was a bond that had changed my view of the world, dulling the colours and sounds of nature. To my eyes, the shades of sunrise and sunset appeared as a dull rusty brown. To my ears, the drone of crickets in the undergrowth pitched too low. To this day, ten years on, I could only imagine the warmth of the sun on my skin, the fresh smell of grass following the rains, and the rich colours of wildflowers.

Overhead I heard the call of a bird. Its pitch was off, but I recognised the hawk before I saw it circling. I stood up and held out an arm, hand clenched into a fist as I let out a shrill whistle. The hawk swooped down in a wide arc, and landed on my outstretched hand. With head cocked, its beady eyes met mine in a familiar exchange.

'Let's fly,' I said, in a tongue that was second nature.

I dipped my arm and pushed it back up, sending the hawk into the air. It took off, gaining speed with the wind behind it, flying high above the grasslands. It was a master of the skies, wings spread, soaring effortlessly on the currents.

'Why do you fly with me?' it said.

I didn't know how I could fly with a bird, or run with a wolf, or leap across trees with a monkey. I had been with animals all my life and had spoken to them long before I would talk to people. Whereas a person would leave you, blame you, hurt you, an animal would not. In comparison, the life of an animal seemed simple and safe; my bond with animals was one I could trust with my secrets and fears. I had spoken with them, lived with them, studied their ways, and over time, they had allowed me to share the most intimate of connections – their bodies. At first, I had thought it was just my imagination, seeing grass whipping past the legs of a deer as it ran, but then came the smell of sodden earth, and the sounds of other running deer charging alongside. I was no longer watching from a distance, I was at one with the deer, running with the herd.

'I fly to be away. Up here everything is simple. Up here the world makes sense.' *Up here I am free of the shadow.* At one with a bird or a deer, any creature, was the only place the shadow could not follow.

I was a passenger on board a bird that flew of its own free will, attune to its senses, yielding to its control. As we soared high and low, I gazed longingly at the view. Seen through the hawk's eyes I saw the world as it should be: the lush green of the grasslands and hillocks marking the landscape, dotted with splashes of colourful wild flowers; the sharp contrast of the grey stone cave and, to the north, the bronze and grey tones of the mountain summits tipped against a bright blue sky. I savoured the crisp colours and fresh aroma in the air, as my gaze lingered south, spying the deep green forest canopy in the distance.

The hawk took a sudden dive. Exhilarated by the rush of moving air, I spied the mouse. Reluctantly I thought back to the cave, preferring not to bear witness to the kill.

3. Wanda

FROM THE MOUTH OF THE cave, I watched the hawk swoop down into the long grass and then fly back up. *Did you catch it my friend?*

Distracted by the sound of soft thudding below, I looked down and saw a familiar face climbing up the hillock towards me. Juna was the father I'd never had; as always, he was a welcome sight.

'I thought I'd find you here,' he said, climbing up over the ledge to sit beside me.

I smiled at him, my gaze lingering on the warmth in his face. Crinkled lines appeared in his dark skin, as his eyes gently narrowed and his lips turned up into a slight smile. My own smile faded; the cold brush on the back of my neck told me the shadow had moved in behind us. Juna didn't see the shadow, no one did, but he knew me, better than most. I turned from his gaze, rested my head on his shoulder, fearful, as always, that he would see what I wanted no one to see. I never told him that I heard the voice of Orag, or that I was cursed by the shadow. It was the thing I feared most, that anyone should believe what I believed: I was evil.

Juna's solid presence was a comfort. The power of the shadow dulled my senses, but I still had my memories. Looking out over the plains, my head nestled against his shoulder, I remembered the freshness of his smell: a complex aroma of woodchip, earth and herbs. He had been my role model, the man who had taught me all he knew about wildlife in the valley. The times we had spent together tracking, taking in injured animals, creating wood carvings of birds, boar and deer, were happy times that seemed so long ago. Ever since marrying my aunt, Ntombi, Juna was too busy to spend much time with me.

'Are you staying tonight?' I asked, hopeful. 'We could go tracking for red deer.'

'No Wanda, I've come to bring you home.'

I lifted my head from his shoulder and stared out at a flock of yellow-throated warblers in the distance.

'I thought I'd stay here a few more nights,' I quietly said.

'You've been gone for weeks,' Juna said. 'You're needed at home.'

Home. It was a long time since Juna's cottage had felt like home, but I couldn't say that to Juna. He was a loyal man, but he wasn't only loyal to me. I couldn't say that Ntombi didn't want me there, couldn't tell him about the bad blood between me and my aunt; that was an unspoken truth that we kept to ourselves.

The warblers were heading south east, flocked in their usual V formation. I watched them disappear into the distance, thinking how I wished Juna had never married my aunt. But then there was Luna.

'Wanda?' Juna said. 'Luna needs you. She's not well.'

'Another nightmare?' I said, my eyes narrowing as I glanced at Juna.

He shook his head. 'She ran away. I think she was looking for you. She was up in the mountains when I finally found her, screaming like a wild thing, making no sense at all. I've never seen her like that when she's awake.'

'Why would she look for me in the mountains?' I asked. It was a place I feared, the origin of the shadow; a place I'd never gone back to ever since I was cursed.

'I don't know.'

'But she's home now,' I said, knowing I would go to her but feeling torn.

'Yes, she's home. And she needs you.'

She needed me and I would go to her, like I always did. As a baby she had cried whenever I left the room, and from the day she started crawling she always came to me. When she was old enough, I had showed her the grasslands and forest, taught her about wildlife as Juna had once taught me. Even the shadow could not dull the happy memories of nights camping out among the trees. But when her nightmares started, things changed. Now, at ten years old, Luna was a complex child.

I was the only one able to wake her from the nightmares; the only one able to calm her down. But it had been years since Ntombi trusted me with her precious daughter. I was sure she blamed me for the way Luna was. I know she thought I was bad, after all, she had never protected me from being beaten as a child. Maybe she was right, maybe I was bad, like a rotten apple. I must be; why else would the shadow have bonded to me?

4. Luna

I KNELT BY THE FIRE, stoking the flames, feeling my mother's eyes on me. Ever since Juna had found me in the mountains, home felt like being trapped in a cage. I had said the name of what I saw on that mountain summit: dragon. Juna didn't see it, and has been whispering with mother about me ever since. Now mother frets and fusses even when I'm just out in the garden.

I poked the biggest log, and watched burning embers splinter and rise. Gazing into the flames, watching patterns come and go in the hot glow, a shape was slowly forming. I inched closer, curious to see again what I had seen the night before. A fiery creature appeared in the flames, small enough that it could have sat in the palm of my hand. With a long, horned tail, spiny wings, and fire spurting from its open jaws, it was a creature of legend. Dragons belonged in tales told from distant lands. So why was I seeing them?

I wasn't afraid of the dragon in the fire. It appeared cute and playful, and was nothing like the monster of my nightmares. Running through the forest, seeing a shadow through the trees overhead, in all the years of having the same nightmare I never saw what was hunting me. Until recently. It was the same fire breathing monster I had seen in the mountains, only that time I was awake. I brushed a finger over the scar on my cheek, remembering the scalding heat of dragon fire.

'Luna?' mother said. 'What are you doing?'

I glanced back out of the corner of my eye and saw mother at the table, watching me closely.

'Nothing.'

I looked back at the fire and rested the poker on the hearth, smiling to see the dragon still in the flames. When I stood up to stir the pot hanging over the fire, I heard mother slicing the loaf of bread. She didn't see what I saw, no one did. I sometimes wondered whether I had a gift, like Wanda, but no one talked about gifts where you see dragons. Either way, it was better not to say anything. Mother was the reason Wanda kept leaving; she didn't like that he had a gift.

'They're back,' mother said; as usual, when speaking of Wanda, her tone was guarded.

I dropped the ladle in the stew and went to the window. Juna was heading up the garden path, closely followed by Wanda. He had been gone too long; the dragons of my nightmares didn't get close when Wanda was around. I forgot I was cross with my cousin for leaving, as I ran for the door, eager to greet him.

Wanda waved when he saw me coming. I went to return his wave but dropped my arm back down by my side and stopped on the path. There was something there, following Wanda, like a shadow walking upright, or was it the ghost of a man? Juna didn't seem to notice as he patted me on the shoulder before walking past. Wanda stopped in front of me, glancing back briefly before resting his gaze on me.

'Aren't you pleased to see me?' he said.

The shadow was at his back. I hesitated before looking at him and nodding. When he put an arm around me, I hugged him back.

'Well, I suppose we should go in,' Wanda said.

He walked ahead but I stayed where I was, watching the shadow follow him. Colours were forming in the grey, slowly revealing a woman. Wanda stopped, looked back and said, 'Are you coming?'

I nodded and walked towards him, eyes on the ghostly woman looking back at me. She was like no one I had seen before, with pale white skin like chalk, silvery blue eyes and hair the colour of fire. When she reached out and put her hand on my arm, her fingers turned to flames but her touch was cool.

'Luna?' Wanda said. 'What is it?'

'Don't you see her?' I said, meeting Wanda's gaze. When I saw the fear in his eyes and clenched jaw, I added, 'Never mind.' If he thought I was seeing things, he would just fret like everyone else.

I looked back at the woman but she was gone, along with the shadow.

5. Wanda

FOR THE FIRST TIME, I was nervous in Luna's presence. She looked straight at the shadow as though she saw it. But if she did, why didn't that frighten her? Her eyes were blood-shot and watery, as though she hadn't slept well in days. I looked at the scar on her cheek, from when she had been burnt in the mountains as a baby. Usually it showed as a patchwork of light brown shades patterned with criss-crossing white lines, in contrast to her warm brown skin. Today the scar was red and inflamed.

We followed Juna into the cottage. Ntombi was sitting by the fireplace, stirring a steaming pot. She looked up when we entered, regarding me with a strained expression in her clenched jaw and narrowed eyes. Juna went to her and kissed her on the forehead. When he pulled back, their gaze held. I turned away, feeling uneasy in her company; few words ever passed between me and my aunt.

I sat down at the table, opposite Luna. Juna brought the pot, slowly followed by Ntombi leaning heavily on her walking stick. Discomfort showed on her face as she sat down, accepting two spoonfuls of remedy Juna gave her. The earthquake that struck the mountains when Luna was a baby had claimed many victims. Ntombi's legs had been so badly crushed, everyone feared she would never walk again. All these years later, she still suffered pain in her legs and was reliant on Juna's potion. Seeing her discomfort, I felt guilty for my ill feeling towards her.

Juna served the soup then reached across, patting me on the shoulder.

'We're glad you're back,' he said.

I looked at him and gave a weak smile, before swallowing my first mouthful.

Ntombi leaned over for the kettle but it was out of her reach and closest to me. Hand poised over my bowl, I waited for her to ask me to pass it, but she didn't. It was always the same, an unspoken tension between us. I passed her the kettle, avoiding her eye.

'Tell Wanda about the mealies, Luna,' Juna said.

Luna swallowed her mouthful, smiled and said, 'You won't believe how high they've grown.'

I looked at her and returned her smile, amused to see the pride on her face. I picked up my spoon, dipped it in the soup, but paused, hand poised. Feeling a brush of cold against the back of my neck, hearing the faint sound of clicking, screeching and humming, my smile faded. I clenched my jaw and tightened my grip on the spoon.

Usually I was alone when the swarming melody rose up out of the shadow, but it had happened before in their company. The first time they heard it, Juna had looked for a swarm, curious to identify a sound he'd not heard before. The source of the shadow's sound remained a mystery. There were times they didn't appear to hear it at all, and times when I knew they did; these days no one spoke during the tense silence, pretending nothing was amiss. Ntombi's stare was fixed on Juna, Juna's eyes glanced from side to side, and Luna was looking at me, one eyebrow raised.

I reached for a slice of bread, tore off a hunk and dipped it into the soup.

'How high?' I said to Luna.

Her eyes gently squinted as she looked at me.

I swallowed the bread and said, 'The mealies. How high have they grown?'

A curious smile spread across her face as she said, 'Nearly as tall as me.'

It took little encouragement for Luna to tell about how well she'd cared for the crop of maize, and the chickens, and beans. With me she was always eager to impress. Her enthusiasm lifted the mood, and in turn the sound from the shadow grew faint until it was quiet.

'The beans will soon be ready to harvest,' Luna said, before swallowing the last spoonful of soup.

'You've watered the crops well,' Juna said.

Luna fell silent. She rested the spoon in the bowl and touched her forearm, frowning as her fingers lingered on her skin as though she could feel something. Slowly, deliberately, she placed both hands flat on the table and raised her gaze to look at Juna.

'They won't need watering when the storm comes.' She glanced towards the window. 'Skies be merciful.'

No one spoke. I stared at Luna, confused by her strange choice of words, spoken with a serious tone of voice, and slightly deeper than she usually spoke. Everything about her appeared odd. She had seemed confused by Juna's words; now, looking through the window, there was sadness in her thoughtful gaze. Even her posture seemed unlike her: sitting with her back and shoulders straight, her arms at perfect right angles resting on the table. She looked as though she was seated at a formal table, rather than with family in her own home.

'There'll be no storm anytime soon,' Juna said, breaking the quiet. 'It's too early for the rains.'

Luna's eyebrows furrowed into a confused frown as she turned to Juna and said, 'What?'

I reached across the table and put a hand over Luna's. 'Luna, are you feeling all right?'

She turned to me, nodded and offered a familiar smile as she said, 'You can help me harvest the beans.'

She picked up her spoon and looked down into her bowl, appearing surprised to find it empty. She rested the spoon back in the bowl.

'It's time for bed, Luna,' Ntombi said, resting her clenched hands on the table.

'Why?' Luna said. 'It's still early.'

'It's not that early,' Ntombi said. 'Besides, you're tired, you need some sleep.' When Luna made no move, Ntombi added, 'Do as I say.'

Luna let out a loud sigh as she pushed her chair back. She turned to me and said, 'You are staying, aren't you?'

I nodded. 'I'll see you in the morning.'

I watched her climb the ladder into the loft.

'I need some fresh air,' Ntombi said.

'Good idea,' Juna said, forcing a smile as he stood up. 'I'll get your chair. We can pick some flowers; this cottage could do with some brightening up.'

'Not tonight,' Ntombi said. 'I think I'll just sit on the bench a while.'

They went out together onto the porch, leaving the door ajar behind them. It had been years since Ntombi had trusted leaving Luna alone with me.

After rinsing the dishes, I climbed the ladder into the loft. Luna was already curled up in bed, softly snoring. I got into my own bed fully dressed and pulled the blanket up to my chin. Aware of the shadow, I turned my thoughts to the hawk.

I WAS WOKEN BY PAINS in my stomach so sharp it made my eyes water. I curled my knees up to my chest, rocking to and fro, wondering what was wrong. My body was clammy with cold sweat as I stared at the moonlight streaking through the shutters. Hearing Luna's quiet moans, I looked over and saw her tossing and turning beneath the sheets. Suddenly, she sat bolt upright, clawing at her nightgown as she screamed in terror. Clutching my stomach, I dragged myself up and staggered across the loft floor towards her.

6. Luna

I was in the sacred forest, standing in the shade of an acatcha tree, waiting for Wanda to return. Clumps of aloe grass grew in the crevices of exposed tree roots, and white speckled panther cap mushrooms littered the ground around my feet. Wanda had taught me all about the forest; I could name many species of plants, animals and birds.

I looked up into the canopy, wondering why I could hear no birdsong. Seeing the sky through tightly woven branches turn dark, I nervously clenched my fists. My heart began beating fast in anticipation of the dragon. I lowered my gaze, suddenly feeling sick. I put my hands on my hips and bent forwards, looking down. I was shocked to see no ground beneath me. The forest floor surrounded my feet, but I was standing over a black hole. I tried to step back but my feet wouldn't move. I suddenly dropped like a stone through a pitch-black sky.

As I fell, tightness in my chest was so intense I couldn't breathe. I gripped my smock as the pain grew sharp and stabbing, until I heard a quick succession of sickening cracks. I watched in horror as my broken, splintered ribs burst out through my chest.

The terror of my ribs cracking followed me into the waking world. My heart was pounding as I sat bolt upright in bed, screaming in agony. I clawed at my chest, then slapped a hand over my burning face where it felt like a red-hot poker was pressing against my cheek. Wanda was there with his hands on my shoulders, trying to soothe me and ease me to lie back down. I lashed out, scrambling free of his grasp, and half ran, half

16

fell down the ladder. I pushed past Juna waiting at the bottom and made for the door, but it was locked. I ran to the window and banged my fists against the shutters, desperate for the cool night air to soothe my burning skin. Feeling hands grip my shoulders from behind, I pulled away. It was the silent part of me that turned and saw the girl held in Wanda's grip.

'Let me go!' the girl cried. 'I've got to get out!'

'Don't fret,' Wanda said. 'It's just a nightmare. You're awake now.'

The girl's screams slowly subsided, but the scar on her cheek began to change. It grew red and inflamed, glowing so bright it appeared like orange light was shining out through the fine lines of the scar. When her head slumped forward, her face was hidden behind her long hair hanging down. There was a moment of silence before the girl looked up, smirking as she met Wanda's eyes.

When she spoke, it was the voice of a stranger speaking through her lips, deep and growling like an old man: 'I see it too; the shadow.'

Wanda clutched hold of his side, wincing as though in pain, staring at the girl as though she was the cause of his pain.

'You're trying to control me,' the growling voice said. 'Stay out of my head.'

Frightened of the unfamiliar voice controlling my body, confused by why the silent part of me existed at all, I reached out to touch the girl's arm. My fingers felt cool skin, my heart started pounding, and my cheek was stinging like an old burn. Back in my body, I slumped forward, resting my head against Wanda's chest.

7. Wanda

No one spoke at breakfast. Ntombi stared anxiously down into her plate, Juna offered the odd forced smile in between mouthfuls, and I watched Luna. She said she had seen the shadow, my curse. Now she appeared tired and listless, sitting with her shoulders slumped as she pushed egg around her plate. I thought back to the night before, and the orange glow shining out from her scar. It had appeared bright even to my eyes and was still red. I had seen her have nightmares before, but nothing like that. Remembering her speak with a deep growling voice, I wondered if my mind was playing tricks.

She pushed her plate aside, looked at me and said, 'Will you come collect the eggs?'

I glanced at Ntombi, expecting her to say something since breakfast wasn't finished, but she didn't look up from her plate. Neither did Juna. I followed Luna outside, away from the cottage where she began searching for eggs among chickens roosting in the bushes.

'Are you feeling all right this morning, Luna?' I asked.

'I suppose,' she said, reaching under a bush and retrieving two eggs.

'I just wondered, after the nightmare you had last night.'

She turned to face me and shrugged her shoulders. 'I've got a headache, that's all.' She put the eggs into the basket and then moved down to the next bush.

I wanted to ask what she remembered, but I didn't: I was afraid she might speak about the shadow again. I glanced behind me, at the shadow lurking close by. All morning Luna had seemed oblivious to it. Maybe

18

she had just been confused, waking from a nightmare but not fully awake; it was possible she'd heard me muttering about the shadow in my sleep. She looked tired, we all did, but apart from that she seemed her usual self.

'What are you doing?' she said, bringing another handful of eggs back to the basket. 'You're supposed to be helping.'

The basket was soon full, so we started on the weeding.

Working together throughout the morning, weeding mealies, milking goats, I forgot my worries and relaxed in Luna's company. We soon fell into our usual play-fighting, chasing each other around the crops.

With a well-aimed shot, dirt hit me in the face. 'I'll get you for that,' I said. I rubbed the grit from my eyes and ran after her. She shrieked as I caught up, laughing as I rubbed dry dirt into her hair.

'What's the joke?' Juna said.

I looked up as he approached carrying a tray of drinks. When Luna saw him, she turned her back and skulked off, disappearing into the long maize. I looked after her, confused, and turned back to face Juna. The tired anxiety in his eyes was a reminder of how I'd felt not long ago. But after spending time with Luna, I'd forgotten my worries.

'Go away, Juna!' Luna shouted out from hiding.

I was shocked. I'd never heard Luna raise her voice to Juna before. Juna said nothing, just fixed me in an anxious stare.

I turned to look into the maize. 'Luna, what's wrong with you? Don't speak to Juna like that.'

She didn't answer.

'Luna?' I tried again, but she didn't move.

Only moments ago, she had been happy in my company. Now she was upset, and angry. Gazing out across the yellow tips of crop, I felt suddenly annoyed. I was scowling when I turned back to face Juna. *Why did you have to come out here?* My thoughts and feelings were confusing, but I kept the scowl for Juna, wishing he would go away. He put the tray down on the ground, turned and walked back to the cottage. I watched the door close behind him, confused by the anger I still felt towards him.

'Let's go for a walk,' Luna said, emerging from hiding. She took my hand and led me out into the plains.

8. Luna

I HAD STARTED THE DAY with a sore head, angry and irritable. But after spending the morning with Wanda my headache was gone. I didn't want Juna, or mother; I wanted Wanda all to myself, at least for a while. His gift meant he was different, like me.

I was happy to get away from the cottage for a while. Out in the grasslands, picking wild flowers in the afternoon sun, it was the furthest I had been from home since Juna had found me in the mountains. Picking purple violets to add to my growing bouquet, I looked over at Wanda snoozing in the grass. He had started the day worried about me. I was sure he would ask me again about the nightmare, but I didn't like to think about it or talk about it. The nightmares were changing; last night's was the most frightening yet.

Wanda stirred as I approached, carrying the flowers. When he sat up in the grass, something appeared behind him. It was the same ghostly shadow I had seen the day before. And as before, colours slowly emerged in the grey, revealing the strange looking woman.

'Don't you see her?' I asked.

Wanda glanced to the side, appearing nervous when he looked back at me.

He hesitated then said, 'See who?'

'She's just there, beside you. The white woman with red hair.'

I stepped towards her, but the colour of her image was fading to grey until she disappeared. I looked at Wanda, expecting to see him watching me, but he was looking beyond me. I turned and saw the girl still standing where I had been only moments ago. I looked down at my hands, seeing my ghostly form, realising the silent part of me had once again left my body. And as before, the girl was oblivious to my presence.

'There is no woman,' Wanda said to the girl.

The girl's eyebrows furrowed into a frown as she dropped the flowers and said, 'Skies be merciful. May the good gifts keep us safe.'

These odd phrases were spoken in a voice that sounded more like a woman than a girl. I walked towards the girl, confused by the vacant look in her eyes as I held out a hand, wanting to reach her. I felt the cool of our touch replaced by the feel of the sun on my skin as I looked out from my body.

'Why are you saying that?' Wanda said.

I stared at him, feeling the urge to cry.

'Something is happening to me,' I said, my voice cracking. 'I don't like it when you leave me.'

Wanda stood up and came towards me, resting a hand on my shoulder. 'I'm right here.'

I KEPT MY ARM LINKED through Wanda's all the way back to the cottage. Once home, mother asked me to help prepare the stew, which I did, with some reluctance. I wanted Wanda to stay close by, but he went outside with Juna.

Once dinner was ready, we sat together at the table. I hadn't eaten much that day but I still wasn't hungry. I spied Juna watching me closely as I pushed food around my plate, and purposely avoided his eye.

He rested his fork down on his plate and asked, 'Are you feeling all right, Luna?'

I nodded. 'I'm just not very hungry.'

Juna cleared his throat, then said, 'Wanda told me what you said, about seeing a woman.'

'What?' mother said. 'What woman?'

My cheeks were burning as I glared at Wanda, but he kept his eyes fixed on his plate.

'Luna,' Juna said. 'Talk to us.'

I didn't answer, nor avert my gaze from Wanda. I had confided in him, and he had told. I was glad I hadn't told him anymore. If they knew the rest, they'd never let me out of the cottage again.

Juna reached over and put his hand on mine. I pulled away, pushed my chair back and stood up.

'There's nothing to talk about,' I said.

'Sit down,' mother said. 'Dinner's not finished.'

'I'm not hungry!'

I turned and went to the loft ladder. I just wanted to be left alone.

9. Wanda

ALL DAY I HAD FELT like I wasn't in control of my own feelings. What Luna felt, I felt, as though somehow my own emotions were mirroring hers. We had always been close, but now it felt like she was inside my head. And I was worried about her. It was the only reason I'd told Juna anything. Now it was me Luna was angry with.

Ntombi was sitting with her head in her hands; Juna was standing behind her, one hand on her shoulder. I looked at them, irritated and restless, feeling a dull ache in my stomach. Life was simpler at the cave, even if it meant I was alone with the shadow. But I was worried for Luna and that left me torn. I didn't speak as I left the table and went outside. Sitting on the bench, I looked up at the moon that was shining bright in a clear night sky.

I could hear Ntombi and Juna's hushed voices from inside the cottage, just whispers until Ntombi raised her voice enough for me to hear her say, 'He's not helping. She's got worse since Wanda came back.'

'That's not true,' Juna said. 'He calmed her down last night. He's the only one who can when she's like that.'

'Maybe,' Ntombi said. 'But why is he telling you about Luna seeing a woman? Why is he making things up about my daughter?'

'How do you know he's making it up?' Juna said. 'If Luna can claim to see a dragon in the mountains, she can say she sees a woman who's not there.'

There was a pause before Ntombi said, 'I'm scared, Juna. I'm scared for my daughter. Wanda's encouraging her and she doesn't need that.

It's not normal what he does: speaking with animals. His gift is a curse and now he's affecting my daughter.'

I put my hands over my ears not wanting to hear more. It wasn't a surprise; I'd heard it before. Ntombi was always looking for reasons to keep me at a distance, afraid I would turn Luna against her, afraid I would reveal how her first husband, Wiseman, used to be beat me, and how she had done nothing to protect me. Worst of all, there was a part of me that wondered whether she was right. After all, I *was* cursed. Was it possible my young cousin had seen the shadow?

The door opened and Juna came out. He sat down next to me on the bench.

'I heard what she said in there,' I said, still looking up at the sky.

'She doesn't mean it, Wanda. She's just worried about Luna.' He paused. 'Come to think of it, you've not been yourself today either.'

I looked down, embarrassed by the thought of how I had behaved towards Juna that morning.

After a moment's silence, he said, 'Why don't you try talking to your aunt?'

'What's the point,' I said. 'She thinks I'm lying.'

'None of us know what to think right now.' He put a hand on my arm. 'You and your aunt, I'll never understand what it is between the two of you.'

My thoughts drifted to childhood, and the day I'd helped myself to a stick of bread in the kitchen. Wiseman had come up behind me, smacked me on the side of the head so hard, I fell, cracking my head against the table before hitting the floor. Ntombi was watching from the corner. She had probably been there the whole time and had done nothing to stop him. I clasped my fingers together, tempted to tell Juna, but I didn't. I never did. I was afraid he wouldn't believe me. I was afraid he loved Ntombi more than he loved me.

I pushed the thought away and sat up straight, folding my arms as I looked at Juna. I was beginning to doubt what was real and what was my imagination, but I was sure the scar on Luna's cheek had been red and inflamed that morning.

'Luna's scar,' I said. 'Tell me how she got it.'

24

'You know how. She was burned by a fire in the mountains.'

'When she was a baby,' I finished. 'But isn't it odd that she was the only one burned?'

'I don't know what you're getting at,' Juna said. 'When the earthquakes hit the mountains, it was chaos. Luna had been separated from your aunt. They were both lucky to survive.'

I didn't know what I was getting at either. Nothing made sense. I turned to face Juna, the man I had always looked up to and admired, and only felt irritated.

THAT NIGHT BEGAN THE SAME as the night before. I was woken by agonising stomach cramps, in time to see Luna sit bolt upright in bed, screaming. When I went to calm her, the lines patterning her mottled scar glowed orange as she fought me off, scrambling down the ladder. The pains in my stomach turned to a dull ache, as I followed to where Luna stood pounding her fists against the shutters, so hard she forced them open. Watched by Juna and Ntombi, I went to stand behind her, nervously placing my hands on her shoulders, softly whispering. Slowly her screams calmed.

I kept my hands on her shoulders, quietly waiting for her to give me a sign that it was over. When the familiar melody of humming, screeching and clicking rose out of the shadow, I clenched my jaw and stared out into the night.

'We all hear it,' Luna said, in the deep growling voice. She turned to face me, head cocked, eyes narrowed. 'And I see it; the shadow, your curse.'

I stepped back, clutching my stomach as sharp stabbing pains returned.

'Luna stop,' I said. 'You are not yourself.'

Her mouth screwed into a smirk, malice shone from her dark eyes, and the scar on her cheek was glowing so bright it looked like a light was shining out from beneath her skin.

'The grace of the temple won't keep you safe,' she said. 'You will all burn in dragon fire!'

'Luna, stop,' Ntombi cried.

Luna's head jerked to the side, as though by an involuntary movement. When she started screaming again, the searing pain in my stomach felt like I was on fire. I doubled over, struggling to catch my breath, and grabbed Luna's arms, desperate for it all to stop. Luna tried pulling away but I gripped her tight.

'Wanda!' Ntombi yelled. 'Juna, get him off her!'

Juna came and grabbed me from behind, pulling me off Luna as her screams turned to cries.

'It's burning!' Luna cried, pressing a hand to her cheek. She ran to her mother, collapsing in Ntombi's open arms.

While Ntombi sat stroking her daughter's hair, Luna's cries slowly calmed and the pain in my stomach eased. When the room fell quiet, Ntombi sat back, inspecting the dark patches on Luna's arms where I had grabbed her. She turned to look at me with accusing eyes.

'You were hurting her,' she said.

'I was just trying to bring her round.'

'Well you didn't have to grab her so tightly,' she said. 'Look at her arms. You can still see your fingerprints on her skin.'

Luna turned to face me, brushing the hair from her face to reveal a hateful look in her staring eyes.

It was the same deep growling voice that spoke: 'He wanted to hurt me. He blames me, but he's cursed by his own shadow.'

'Oh please stop, Luna,' Ntombi said, with fear in her eyes as she sat back from her daughter.

Luna stood up, turning her back on her mother and fixing her eyes on me. Screeching, humming and clicking rose out of the shadow as she slowly stepped towards me. Her movements were stiff and her eyes dark, as the growling voice spoke to me:

'It is your curse we can hear. The shadow bound to the dragon, bound to you. You want to curse me, control me, but you are too weak.' She paused in front of me, holding me in a challenging stare, before turning away and climbing the ladder into the loft.

The shadow's song continued, as the rest of us were left staring at one another.

'What is that sound?' Ntombi said. 'What's wrong with you? What are you doing to my daughter?'

'Ntombi!' Juna said.

'No,' she said. 'I won't stop. There's something wrong with my daughter and this isn't helping.'

Seeing the accusation in my aunt's face, in that moment I hated her. 'You never wanted me near your precious daughter. You're so afraid I'll tell her what a bastard her real father is, and how *you* treated me when I was a child.'

'Oh, get out!' she yelled.

'Gladly!' I turned and left, slamming the door behind me.

10. Suni

MY MOTHER HAD BEEN A dreamwalker, a gift passed from mother to daughter. We were separated for years before she died, but she had always been able to reach me in my dreams. It was only after she died, ten years ago, that I realised the gift had found its way to me.

I see the mists of *Serafay* at the edge of my dreams, mists only the dead or a dreamwalker can know. How to navigate the mists is still a mystery even to me; it just is. Sometimes I think the destination lies rooted in desire. My mother had missed me, worried for me, a longing that had led her to me. My own nightly ventures took me to the dreams of my young friend, Wanda; a gifted boy I had known since he was an infant. Ours was a bond formed during an extraordinary journey we had once shared.

Much had changed since then, and the distance between us meant I couldn't visit often. A boy gifted to speak the tongues of animals, he lived among wildlife in the valley beyond the mountains, while I had returned to my coastal hometown. I thought of him often, worried about him. I was aware that his relationship with Ntombi, my old friend, was not as it should be. I was thankful for my gift, reassured by my visits into his dreams.

ONE NIGHT I CLOSED MY eyes and drifted from the waking world, descending into sleep. Random colours and images of everyday life came and went, but I drifted on through until the colours drained to grey, and I was standing before the wall of mist. I stepped in, abandoning caution, and surrendered to my gift.

28

In the thick grey haze, the air was still and cool. I walked blind, deeper into the mist where ghosts crossed my path. They appeared oblivious to me, sometimes walking straight through me, leaving the cold of their presence lingering on my skin. Whilst my mother was at peace, ghosts aimlessly wandering *Serafay* had mournful, despairing eyes.

I felt a change in the air; a slight breeze brushed against my hand. I held out my hands, finding the direction, and turned to walk into the breeze. It was always the same, the mist showing me the way. The breeze grew stronger the further I went into the tunnel of moving air that was hidden from the dead. Among the swirling tones of grey, a window of colour appeared up ahead. I walked towards it, unsure of where it would lead. The only certainty was the dreamer; it was always Wanda I came to when I walked out of *Serafay*.

I stepped out of *Serafay* to find myself in Juna's cave. Wanda was there, his back to me, sitting with legs dangling over the overhanging shelf, head cocked as he looked out over the grasslands. I stepped around the burnt-out fire and went to him. The sun was shining down as I stood next to him on the ledge, but the cold of *Serafay* lingered.

I crouched down and looked at his face. He never saw or heard me in the dream world. Sometimes I'd see him appear unresponsive to anything as he gazed intensely into space. This time was different; only the whites of his eyes were showing. I put a hand on his arm, reassured by the warmth of his body that felt like a shock against the cold of mine, and looked out across the landscape. *Where are you?* Startled by a shrill call overhead, I glimpsed a circling hawk, before *Serafay* came to claim me.

I OPENED MY EYES, STILL feeling the cold of *Serafay* as I re-entered the waking world. Lying on my side, watching the flickering glow of the candle still burning, the musty smell of the cellar was a comfort; the familiar aroma of home. I turned onto my back, pulled the blanket up to my chin, and looked at Zandi sleeping beside me. After years living together as lovers and friends, she was my constant and I hers.

We had built our cottage over the foundations of my childhood home, replicating the design of a single room with a grass roof built over the original cellar. Years ago, the old regime that had once governed the land had burnt my home to the ground, intending to trap me and my mother, Mata, inside. Witch hunts no longer happened since the fall of the King, but sleeping upstairs still gave me nightmares of the fire.

The candle crackled, almost burned out. I turned back onto my side, facing the steps, and closed my eyes, thinking of evenings spent with my mother in the cellar, reciting herbal lore and preparing ointments and potions. Ten years on and I still missed her. She had taught me so much; I only wish we'd had more time.

Remembering my mother was a comfort that never lasted, since it always led to the man responsible for tearing us apart, King Rhonad. The King had been my enemy, but when I had finally come face to face with him, I realized the evil plaguing our beloved land delved deeper than just one man. Gogo, wise woman and my great-grandmother, spoke of an ancient darkness dwelling deep in the mountains. The miners digging for crystals had delved too deep. I had seen it on that fateful day: an evil spirit looked out through the eyes of Rhonad's rotting body, and spoke its name, Orag, on the King's foul breath. The possessed King had died in a fire of his own making, but the dark spirit rose free from the flames. Now I feared the spirit of Orag lurked in the shadows.

Restless, I opened my eyes, and pulled the blanket aside, careful not to wake Zandi as I sat on the edge of the bed. Sipping from a mug of water, I thought of Wanda's staring eyes in the dream, and the hawk, circling overhead. He was a boy gifted to speak the tongues of animals, a gift that had seen the return of the Mantra. The only other person I knew to have possessed the same gift was the King. It was an unsettling thought; Gogo had once warned me about Wanda, describing his gift as one that carried shades of light and dark. At the time I had rejected any notion of Wanda, an innocent child, being compared to the King, but the King had once been just a child too.

'Suni?' Zandi said.

I turned to see her rub sleep from her eyes and said, 'Go back to sleep.'

She sat up to lean on her elbow. 'Another dream?'

I nodded.

She reached out and put a hand on my shoulder. 'You're cold. Come back under the blanket.'

'I can't sleep. I'll go upstairs. I didn't mean to wake you.'

She sat up and put her arms around my waist, resting her chin on my shoulder, pressing her cheek against mine. I leaned into her, savouring the feel of her soft skin.

'What is it?' she said. 'Is it Wanda?'

She was accustomed to my dreamwalking.

I prized her arms loose and shuffled back into bed. She scooped me up into her outstretched arm, pulling me in closer.

'There was something different about him,' I said, nestling my head against her shoulder. 'I saw him, but it was like he wasn't there. I don't know, I just feel like he's changing.'

'He is changing,' she said. 'He's becoming a young man.'

'But what if it's more than that. Sometimes I wonder how powerful his gift is.'

She kissed the crown of my head then said, 'You worry too much. You're just missing him, that's all. We're going to the valley in a few days. You'll feel better after you've seen him again.'

11. Suni

AFTER AN EARLY BREAKFAST, I set off with Zandi through the back streets of town. The sun was rising but the cool of the night still lingered. By the time we reached the crossroads, most homes still had their shutters closed, but a few were stirring.

'See you later,' Zandi said, kissing me quickly on the cheek.

I held onto her hand and pulled her in closer, planting a soft lingering kiss on her lips. When I drew back, I smiled to see the sparkle in her eyes.

'See you later,' I said with a smile.

I lingered on the corner, watching her familiar boyish swagger as she headed in the direction of the river. Armed with a bow and her arrows strapped across her back, I was as proud of her today as I was when we had first met.

Zandi had once been my mentor, training me to join the keepers, teaching me the art of archery and much more besides. Now, each morning she remained hopeful for more volunteers to train, but the town wasn't forthcoming in offering up themselves or their children. The keepers came from the sacred forest in the valley beyond the mountains, a place that had once been deemed an enemy of the town. Despite the keepers now being the town's main defence, and the fact that ten years had passed, they were still mostly treated as outsiders.

I turned, heading in the direction of school. My mornings began with teaching of a different kind.

Formal teaching had long been abandoned and the school transformed into a weekly meeting place for the town council. Aside from that, the building was largely unused, except for the storytelling sessions I ran before market. Many were stories Mata had told me as a child, but some were my own. Stories were my weapon against ignorance, my hope that the next generation might do different than the last.

I rounded the high walls enclosing the old school yard and arrived at the metal gate. Reaching for the latch I stopped, hearing a whimpering cry. I looked down at the basket propped against the wall, and carefully lifted the lid to find a baby monkey crouched inside. With coarse, black fur and bushy tail like a giant tassel tipped with white, it looked to be a tufted tamarin. I picked up the basket, carried it into the yard, and rested it in the shade of the palm tree.

It wasn't the first orphan I'd found, and it wouldn't be the last. The King's reign had been long; a suffering dictatorship that banned free thought. Now we were left with generations of people who had no understanding and little regard for the natural world. Since the earthquakes along the mountain ridge ten years ago, none had dared venture down into the mines. Without crystals to trade, and the mountain passes clear to cross, the valley was falling prey to poaching. Animals of all species were killed, tufted tamarins for their fur. Surviving infants were sold as pets, though they were soon abandoned and left to die. This one was weak. Wanda was the best chance it had; he had successfully introduced many orphans back into the forest.

Hearing the chatter of approaching children, I went to greet them at the gate. One boy, Dani, was further behind than the rest, closely followed by his father. He ran for the gate but I held out an arm to stop him.

'Please Miss,' Dani said, red faced and flustered.

'What harm can it do?' I asked his father.

'There's nothing he needs to learn from you,' he said, scowling as he gripped his son's shoulders before marching him back down the street.

My stories respected the old ways of the Mantra, ideas that too few in Shendi had adopted. Many still claimed they didn't believe in the Mantra,

33

some among them (and I suspected Dani's father) topped up their living by poaching.

I closed the gate behind me and joined the children gathered around the basket in the shade of the tree. Nura was already up in the branches, picking dates. She climbed down, pockets bulging, and took out a handful as she sat next to the monkey.

'Is the baby an orphan?' she asked, peeling back the skin of a date and breaking off a chunk of flesh.

'I think so,' I said, smiling to see the monkey feed from her hand.

'Can we have the story of the lions, today?' another girl asked. 'The one about why they live on the mountains.'

'Not today, Maya,' I said. 'Today I'm going to tell you the story of the north wind.'

Silence fell as I began:

'High above the ocean was the home of the north wind; sea blue was all it had ever known. There were passing ships whose sails it toyed with, but apart from that, the days brought nothing new. The south wind teased it, boasting of having been to distant lands. Longing to see land for itself, the north wind ventured far over the waves, further than it had ever been before; until in the distance it caught its first ever glimpse – land!

'It rushed over the water, eager to explore, danced over surf as the waves leapt ashore, whipped through the riverbank reeds, travelling inland, finally reaching golden terrain. High and low it soared, eager in its search for more, but north, south, east and west, nothing stirred on the dry ground below. On it went, but the force of its gale was slowing, choked with sand whipped up from the desert. The north wind climbed high, trying to see beyond, but there was nothing but sand baking under the hot sun. Disappointed, the north wind turned, eager to feel fresh sea air.

'But the north wind never forgot the land, and every so often it returned, looking hopefully out from the shoreline. One day it saw clouds appear in the clear blue sky, the next it saw the rains. For long days and nights, the downpour continued, and the north wind watched and waited. Slowly, among the golden landscape, patches of green began to sprout, and among the tender vegetation, movement stirred. When the rain finally stopped, the north wind turned its back on the sea and whistled through the riverside reeds, racing inland.

'Gently it blew through tender shoots and soared high through branches of trees. The desert had sprung to life and, no longer blinded by sandstorms, the north wind roamed far to investigate. It whistled over the tails of burrowing rodents, brushed over the long ears of furtive hare, climbed high over rock and boulder, around thorny bush, gracing the bristling black tufts of the mountain lions' ears. Up, up and over the highest mountain peaks it soared; rushing between the legs of a herd of grazing deer, through long grass and wild flowers the colours of the rainbow. Speeding over grassy plains, the wild north wind raced on. Until it met with trees, more trees than it could ever have imagined. The sacred forest with its thick green canopy and strong boughs tamed the north wind, and from that day a gentle breeze hangs over the forest: the north wind, peeking through the branches to marvel at all the creatures that live there.'

'Do you think the north wind has seen the Mantra?' Maya asked with wide eyes.

'I expect so,' I said.

'My mother says there's no such thing,' Yolan said, confusion on his young face. 'She says the rains returned, but the land is still cursed. My father's mealies are being eaten by a plague of mealworms. And there's blight in the next field.'

These days failing crops were a common occurrence, a fact used to aid the argument of non-believers.

'I'm sorry to hear about your father's crops,' I said. 'But blight and mealworms don't mean the Mantra isn't real. It's our Great Spirit, the spirit of this land. I've seen it with my own eyes.'

Unlike Yolan, Maya came from a family of firm believers. 'What does it look like?' she asked.

I gave the answer I always gave: 'The Mantra created all the creatures of our land, and it wears the face of every one of them.'

'Can it look like a lion?' she asked.

'Yes.'

'And a bird?'

'Yes. And a deer, and a hare, and a monkey.' I reached into the basket for the monkey, lifted it out and nestled it in the crux of my elbow. 'The Mantra has brought life back to this land, and so we must respect it. And to respect the Mantra means respecting the animals. If we don't, the Mantra might leave again, and then we'll all suffer the drought.'

'Never mind the drought,' Roja, an older boy said. 'My mother says the streets are haunted and it's the dead bringing disease.'

Whilst I didn't believe ghosts roamed our streets, it was true many suffered a strange affliction; my own father was among them. I stared silently at the children, at a loss for how to explain what plagued our land.

12. Suni

I WAVED THE LAST OF the children off then crossed the street to where Zandi was waiting with the mule and cart, already loaded for market.

'You're early,' I said.

'Yes, well, no volunteers showed.' She shrugged. 'I'm starting to wonder why I bother.'

'Don't give up on them,' I said. The townspeople were stubborn; many had dark pasts, but they were still my people. One day I hoped Zandi might feel the same.

'I haven't yet, have I?' she said. 'After all, it's only been ten years of trying to get them on side!'

The monkey let out a whimpering cry. Zandi looked at the basket I had clutched under my arm.

'What have you got there?' she said, lifting the lid and peering in. 'Damn poachers.' She gently closed the lid. 'We should start stringing them up.'

'If only it was that easy.'

'It looks like it's only a couple of weeks old,' she said. 'Do you think it will survive a trek over the mountains?'

'It has to. It needs to be back in the forest, and Wanda's the best chance it's got.'

'Maybe we should bring the visit forward,' she said. 'Set off early tomorrow.'

I lifted the basket into the cart, wedging it safely between rolls of mats and said, 'We're on watch tonight. Maybe if it's quiet…'

'I wouldn't count on it.' She tugged at the reins, moving the mule on. 'A ship arrived last night with green sails; no one's seen it before.'

We turned a corner, into a street where houses had chicken feet hanging on the doors.

Zandi clicked her teeth in annoyance. 'I swear more of those things go up every day.'

'People are scared,' I said. 'Even the children are talking about blight in the fields and ghosts bringing disease.'

'Superstition,' she said. 'I mean, who ever dreamt up chicken feet being able to ward off evil! In any case, dead crops don't mean this place is haunted.'

'You might be right, but it's easy for people to believe in ghosts when so many lost their lives in the mines and the palace.'

'Ten years ago!' she said. 'If there were such things as ghosts, which there isn't, why wait ten years to come back and haunt us?'

But I feared ten years made no difference to the spirit, Orag.

Gogo had once prophesised two possible destinies: the return of the Mantra, or a breaking of the world as the dark spirit awakened. The Mantra had returned, but not before the power of Orag sent earthquakes ripping through the mountains. The mountains had remained calm for ten years, but was the ancient darkness sleeping? *Blessed be the return of the Mantra. Blessed be the return of the rains.* Mata's prayer. But could the grace of the Mantra keep our land safe?

Zandi had been there and seen what I had seen. All the keepers had. But the path of a keeper did not include believing in spirits or dwelling on the old ways. And so, I kept my thoughts to myself. It wasn't the spirit of Orag causing the concerned look on Zandi's face, as she slowed to a stop at the crossroads.

'Why don't we go the long way round?' she said, reaching for my hand. She always did try avoiding Fazi, my father.

'There's no need, I'm fine.' I squeezed her hand. 'Have you got the poultice?'

'Yes, and bread.'

I smiled, grateful for the support despite her reservations. She clicked her tongue and tugged on the reins, leading the mule on our usual route.

I didn't know Fazi when I was growing up: he was away working at the mines. When I finally met him, I realised he was as corrupt as the rest who worked for the King. For long enough I didn't want to know him, but he worked on gaining my trust and finally I let him into my life. In the end he broke my heart, choosing the same fate as the rest: most of the surviving men from the mines and palace were now known as outcasts.

After the fall of the King's reign, powers of the old regime were stripped back. The keepers had helped. With the truth of their corruption exposed, men who had once served the King retreated to the shadows. In the beginning they had camped out on the banks of the estuary, where shady deals were made with sea traders after dark. But when the keepers set up guard along the shore at night, the outcasts were moved on.

After that, the health of the former King's servants fell into a rapid decline. They were free to fish in the day but they showed no interest, and refused offerings of food. Before long, they were grey-faced and undernourished, rambling to themselves as they scratched like dogs with fleas, until deep sores pitted their skin. Fights often broke out between them, seemingly over nothing. The townspeople kept their distance, fearing a contagious disease that sent the afflicted mad. Whatever the cause, it only seemed to affect the outcasts.

Up ahead, a fight was brewing. After some shoving and pushing, one man grabbed the other's hair and smashed his head into a wall.

'Give me it!' he yelled.

The ruckus brought more outcasts from out of the shadows, encroaching on the two men like stray dogs hunting. From across the street, I saw Fazi among the gaunt faces. I went towards him, taking the bread and poultice, but he ignored me and went to walk on past. I put a hand on his arm to stop him and received his usual response.

'What do you want?' he said, shaking me off.

I shoved the bread and jar of poultice into his hands. 'To give you this.'

'Coins are what I need,' he said, dropping the bread. He kept the poultice. Half-starved, covered in sores, the ointment would at least ease the itching.

I turned away and returned to Zandi.

'I wish you could just forget about him,' she said. 'I can't stand the way he treats you.'

'I know,' I said, touching her arm. 'I just can't help wondering what's wrong with him, what's wrong with all of them.' I glanced back at the crowd of scrapping outcasts. 'Sisile thinks it might be black water pox. It explains the itching and the madness, but I saw an outcast peeing the other day and his water wasn't black.'

13. Suni

NEWS OF THE SHIP HAD brought traders out early to market. By the time we arrived at the square, most of the stalls were already set up. Trade amongst ourselves was mostly bartering, but some sea traders brought gold coins. In anticipation of a prosperous day, stalls were organised with the best of the wares kept back for the sea traders. On our stall that meant the biggest baskets, good for storing grain on long voyages.

Once the cart was unloaded and our wares organised, I rested the basket with the monkey inside under the cart for shade, and sat down at my loom. Weaving was a trade passed down by my mother. Criss-crossing grass reeds under and over, my thoughts drifted to Mata: the feel of her brushing my hair; the way she tapped the teaspoon three times after stirring; and her musty smell as she worked long into the evening mixing potions.

'That looks like trouble,' Zandi said.

I looked up and saw Chad, an experienced keeper, walk by, heading towards a rowdy gathering of traders and sailors. Seeing Sisile, my mother's old friend, confronting a sailor in the middle of the commotion, I got up and went towards them.

'Who did you get this from?' Sisile said, grappling with the sailor for the animal skin he had bundled under his arm.

'What's it to you, old woman?' he said, batting her hands away.

Sisile jabbed his foot with her walking stick, distracting him as she snatched the fur. She held it up, revealing the skin of a lesser-spotted cat.

As Chad hauled the sailor away, my gaze rested on Tilli, sitting nearby brewing a pot of tea over hot coals. She was the only one who hadn't looked up throughout the altercation. It wasn't like her. Selling tea was a hard way to make a living, but she often made a decent day's takings with her gregarious nature and outgoing banter. I noticed her bulging purse before she tucked it into her cleavage. Usually she kept it tied to her belt. When I went towards her, she glanced at me out of the corner of her eye, before staring down at the glowing coals.

'Tilli?' Her cheeks flushed red, but she didn't answer. 'Why?' I said.

She looked up, scowling. 'Don't judge me. What choice do I have? Mistress of a dead guard with three sons to feed. Poaching's the only way I can survive. I worked years in that brothel, but what do I have to show for it? His wife got all the help; I was left with nothing.'

Exploitation had been central to the King's power, something many women and children had been forced to experience first-hand, including me. Tilli had been sold by her father to the brothel at fourteen, and housed as a mistress at sixteen. The brothel had been out of sight, but living as a mistress in town, raising three illegitimate children, her family had shunned her. Her only option was to scratch a living as a tea seller. In the beginning the council had been able to help with food, but with the onset of blight, generosity had diminished.

'Poaching's not the answer,' I said. 'Think where we'll be if the Mantra leaves; we'll all suffer the drought.'

'Superstition!' came a voice from behind. It was Nero, a farmer. 'This land is cursed, worse than it ever was.'

His wife, Fashmi, joined in: 'Our crops are being killed off by blight. And for all we know, the disease on the streets is catching.'

'Some say it's the dead come back bringing the blight,' another voice said.

'Or keepers from the witch valley.'

I looked for the speaker but couldn't see him in the crowd. Instead, I was relieved to see Sunette, Juna's mother and a loyal ally, pushing her way towards me. But she was closely followed by an angry Patsy and her daughter, Vikki.

'I've been looking for you,' Patsy said, waving a finger at me.

'What do you want, Patsy?' Sunette said, holding a protective arm in front of me.

'The truth,' Patsy said, fixing her stare on me. 'You owe us that.'

Patsy had been a loyal follower of the King, and over the years had made it clear how she felt about those who had overthrown him. She wasn't the only one. Bad blood in the town ran deep. We had tried reason, and understanding: people on both sides had suffered; when the quakes destroyed the mines, Patsy's husband had died.

'Just take it easy,' Sunette said.

Patsy kept her stare fixed on me. 'All these years you've said we were wrong, that the King was wrong. You've got over half the town believing what you say. But you're a liar. The people of the valley are witches, and you're shacked up with one!'

'Why can't you just leave things alone?' I said. 'After everything we've all been through, we need to work together.'

'Because it's happening again,' Vikki said, clutching her mother's arm. 'We just came back from the mountains, visiting the place my dad died. There was a wild girl up there, screaming about a dragon! She had a burnt face, scarred and mad like a witch.'

I was stunned. *Surely they can't be talking about Luna?*

'She almost brought the mountain down with her spells,' Patsy said. 'We were nearly killed in the landslide.'

'What *are* you talking about?' Sunette said. She thought of Luna as her granddaughter. 'You escaped a landslide but you're not seriously telling me you're afraid of a young girl.'

Patsy fell quiet for a moment, her eyes narrowing as she looked at Sunette. 'That's right, I forgot your son's over there. Is he shacked up with one too? Is that the reason you're always defending them?'

'You don't know what you're talking about,' Sunette said.

There was a silent stand-off before Patsy smirked, turned her back, and led her daughter away.

'What was that all about?' I said, putting a hand on Sunette's shoulder.

She turned to face me. 'Even if it was Luna she saw, I wouldn't pay any mind to Patsy's account.'

43

'Agreed. But a landslide? There haven't been any landslides since the earthquakes.'

Sunette had been there ten years ago, when the spirit of Orag rose from the ashes to return to the mountains. As earthquakes ripped through the summits, the thought I had back then remained today: *the dead can't die.*

14. Luna

LYING IN THE GRASS AT the edge of the maize crop, staring up at the sky, I felt anger simmering in my belly. Wanda leaving had left the atmosphere in the cottage thick with tension. Every cross word spoken, every hateful feeling shared, lingered in the air like a bad smell.

Chunks of my memory were missing, but I remembered Wanda's public announcement about my real father. It wasn't what he had said that hurt: as far as I was concerned, Juna was the only father I had. But if the man was such a bastard, couldn't Wanda have picked a better moment to let me know?

I brushed a hand over my arm, remembering the white woman's cool touch. Wanda was the person I thought I could trust above everyone, but he had betrayed me in more ways than one. It was the shadow bound to him that the white woman had appeared from, yet he had talked about me to Juna as though I was mad.

I didn't know what was happening to me. The nightmares, the visions, the memory lapses… It was like trying to fit a puzzle together with pieces missing. Somehow, Wanda was connected. I was sure he could help me fill the missing pieces, but he had left me. I was tired of being afraid and misunderstood. Now there was no one I could trust to understand my secret. I was starting to think my visions of the dragon were the only thing left I could rely on.

I searched for it now, in the shape of slow-moving clouds, and saw the vague outline of the beast slowly form. The harder I focused, the shape grew more defined, until the long sweeping tail, arched spiny wings, and angular head dominated the sky. As white clouds turned grey and the sky grew dark, I felt warm inside, like a fire lighting in my belly.

15. Wanda

SITTING ON THE OVERHANG AT the mouth of the cave, I looked at the hawk perched on my clenched hand and said in its tongue, 'I don't belong there anymore. I'm wild like you.'

The hawk didn't answer as it ruffled its wing feathers, eager to hunt. I swung my arm up, releasing the hawk, and felt the power in its beating wings. With the sun in our sights we soared so high, trees appeared to fit in our talons. Scanning the landscape, spying a running track in the grass, we circled, slowly closing the net on a young hare fixed in our sights.

'Are you going to leave?' the hawk said, impatient for the taste of fresh blood.

No. This time I would stay; I was wild now.

The hare sat upright on its hind legs, poised, ears pricked, before making a sudden dash. Wind roared past our face as we dived down on target, sinking our extended talons deep into our quarry. It was still alive when the first of its flesh was torn free. I felt its horror in the pounding of its heart, until it stopped. But I had no pity, only hunger for the steaming blood and soft flesh. *I am wild now.*

'This meal is mine,' the hawk said, pushing me into the far recesses.

AS NIGHT FELL, I HUDDLED against the wall of the cave, staring into darkness. I had stayed for the kill, tasted the warm flesh and rich blood of a living creature. With the memory of fresh blood still lingering on my tongue, I felt ashamed. It was natural for a hawk, but not for a man.

Listening to the shadow's song echoing around the cave, I was haunted by the thought I was evil. There was nowhere to hide, no hiding from myself, no respite to be found even in my dream:

> Standing in the mouth of the cave, I held an arm aloft. The hawk flew down and landed on my clenched hand; it had always trusted me. *I am not your friend.* I curled my thumb over its talons and squeezed, blood dripping from my hand where its claws pierced my skin. It flapped its wings, looking at me with startled eyes. I grabbed it with my other hand and clasped my fingers around its neck, gripping tight as it tried to peck. Its cries were angry and shrill as I knelt down and clamped it between my knees. I smoothed down its ruffled feathers, my hand lingering to feel the pulse in its neck.
> 'Let me go,' it said.
> 'It's your fault,' I said through gritted teeth, as I picked up a rock. 'You made me hungry for the kill.'
> There was horror in its eyes before I smashed the rock into the hawk's skull.

I WOKE, FEELING MY SKIN doused in a cold sweat. The cave was bathed in the first light of dawn, but its glow was masked by the looming shadow. The dream was still vivid in my mind. *I am cursed with evil. I don't belong in this world.* But I feared I wasn't the only one.

Luna.

CLEAR SKIES HUNG OVER THE valley as I set off to find my cousin. But rounding a hillside, I saw dark clouds gathered in the sky over the cottage. Luna was in the garden, her hair blowing back in wind that only appeared to blow around the vicinity of the cottage. As though oblivious to the strange weather, she threw handfuls of corn to the chickens scratching around her feet. She saw me watching and started to raise an arm as though about to wave, but stopped and dropped it back by her side. She was wild like me, a mouse and a hawk rolled into one. Sometimes she hated me, sometimes she needed me, but today she was undecided.

Ntombi's face appeared in the window. Soon after, the door opened and Juna came out. He glanced across in my direction but gave no further acknowledgement.

'Luna, come inside,' he called. 'Your mother wants to speak to you.'

Luna hesitated, eyes on me, before she turned and followed Juna into the cottage.

16. Suni

LATER THAT DAY, AS EVENING fell, Zandi and I headed through the quiet streets, armed with bows and arrows for our night patrol. Only the distant voices of quarreling outcasts, and the odd yowl and bark of stray cats and dogs broke the silence.

Emerging from the back streets, we approached the river that was covered in a blanket of thick mist bathed in moonlight. The mist was a binding spell woven by the elders of the sacred forest, and served as a barrier against invasion. It had once been laid across the mountain summits to stop the King's hoards crossing into the valley. But times had changed and Gogo now preached of a common enemy: darkness encroaching from the seas under cover of night. Ruthless pirates were no stranger to our shores: knowing my great grandmother, the faceless enemy she spoke of did not come in the form of rag tag men.

The waterway stretched from the sea's estuary, cutting through the desert downstream to the narrow tributaries tipping the southern horizon. The mist obscured the seascape, but the murmur of waves lapping the shore was soothing. The sea was a place of safety; my mother had found refuge there; and the sanctuary of the Mantra had been a mystical place in the middle of the ocean. I recalled my own journey out into open waters, and the extraordinary creatures I had seen. I often wondered what lands lay beyond the watery horizon.

Two figures emerged from the mist: a young keeper, Alanda, was frogmarching a soaking wet outcast up the bank.

'Get out of here!' Alanda said as they reached the top of the bank. She shoved him forward and aimed an arrow at his chest. He skulked off in the direction of town, scowling as he passed us.

'Chad caught him swimming for the estuary,' Alanda said, as we approached. 'I don't know why he bothered; got bit for his troubles. We're supposed to be guarding against sea-folk coming to shore, but more often than not it's one of these filthy outcasts heading out to sea, boat or no boat. Why should we care?'

'He should have let him drown,' Zandi said. She looked at me and added, 'Well, sorry, but Alanda's got a point.'

They both had a point, but my father was among those they'd happily see drowned. With the arrival of the mist, and keepers guarding the shores at night, the mad affliction among the outcasts had only worsened. Increasing numbers had been caught trying to swim out to sea; some had disappeared altogether, onto pirate ships infamous for their trade in slaves. Why any would choose the life of a slave was still a mystery. The ship with green sails was still anchored out at sea. Traders by day turned into pirates at night, or worse, if Gogo was right.

'There was a time when this town killed anyone they didn't like,' I said. 'Thankfully those days are gone. Besides, the outcasts aren't harming anyone but themselves.'

Alanda said, 'Well if you ask me, we ought to be in the forest taking down poachers, or, better still, patrolling the mountains and stopping them from crossing in the first place.'

'The Gogo wants us here,' I said, unsure of my own argument.

'To prevent against darkness coming in from the seas,' Alanda said, her voice purposefully croaking to imitate an old woman.

'All right, Alanda,' Zandi said. She was used to dealing with her former trainee's rebellious streak.

'Well it's your problem now,' Alanda said. 'My shift has ended.'

It wasn't the first time I'd heard Gogo's wisdom questioned out loud, and I had nothing to say in its defence. But as we walked into the spellbound mist with bows and arrows poised, I felt protected by the wisdom of the elders.

I closed my eyes: sight was of no use in the mist. Only by unlocking a hidden sense, could a keeper find their way and guard against intruders. I freed my mind of all thought and looked into the abyss, a place of pure void. Echoes of the first light revealed themselves to me, like stars in a night sky. One shone brighter than the rest. I focused on it, felt the familiar tingling sensation flow across my face, through my body, down the reach of my limbs. My hands were gripping the bow and arrow, but my fingers felt gritty sand, rough stone, prickly reeds and cool flowing water. Like a map in my mind's eye, I saw my surroundings revealed in colour: the heat of my companions showed as red and orange; water, rocks and reeds appeared as shades of cool blue. My own form was its unusual pale yellow, cool as it had always been. The spell-bound mist was not the same as *Serafay*, but the weaves bore a resemblance that my gift as dreamwalker recognised.

Guided by my hidden sense, I safely navigated the rough terrain. There were six of us on patrol, recognisable by our stealthy movements and postures armed with bows. Well trained to work the area, we took our positions: three posts guarded the shoreline while three assumed a defensive line, spanning the mist. I took my place in the line, closest to the water as we moved in silent unison upstream towards the estuary.

Our hidden sense was as aware of subtle changes as it was of obvious sounds. The gentle rush of the river was a constant backdrop, and the ripples of water showed as patterns of cool blue, fanning as they flowed downstream. Rhythmic splashes of water followed by heavy gasps were instantly out of place.

'Psst,' I whispered through my teeth, alerting the other keepers.

Behind closed eyes I watched the changing patterns of rippling water, then saw the cool blue of two canoes filled with the red heat of six bodies.

'That's far enough,' Chad called out.

Paddles paused, mid-air, bringing a moment of relative quiet, before a man's voice answered, 'Who's there?'

'Keepers of this land,' Chad said. 'It's forbidden to come to our shores at night. Turn back and you'll come to no harm.'

A streak of blue came whooshing through the air in Chad's general direction. The assailant was blinded by mist and the knife easily missed its target, landing in the ground some distance away. I trained an arrow on the canoe closest to shore, let it loose and heard the thud as it sank into the wooden bow.

'Consider that a warning shot,' I said.

There was fumbling in the boat as the men scrambled back.

'Easy,' one of the sailors said. 'We only came to trade.'

'There's nothing you need to be trading at night,' Chad said.

'The outcasts among you wouldn't agree,' another voice said, ending with a mocking laugh. 'You want us to go, fine, we'll go, for now. But we'll be back.'

Paddles pushed down into the water. As they headed back upstream, a man's voice called out, 'You're out here seeing off sea folk, when you should be sorting out trouble in your own town. This place is turning into the next rat-infested port of Evren!'

The sound of laughter drifted away into the night.

'What did he mean by that?' Chad said.

'No idea,' I said. 'I've never heard of the place. In any case, this town is hardly rat infested.'

'I can't understand why they keep coming here at night,' Zandi said. 'It's not as if the outcasts have anything to trade.'

We fell silent until Chad said, 'We'd better get into position. They could be back.'

THE NIGHT WORE ON, UNEVENTFUL, until I paused, detecting a change. The ebb and flow of the tide sounded strangely distant; the tones of cool blue water appeared masked by a silvery veil. I was startled by a cold chill brushing the back of my neck. My hidden sense left me, leaving me blind in the mist.

I turned around, confused, and saw weaves unravel in the mist, leaving a clear gap like a window into another world. I was awake, but it felt like dreamwalking, seeing Wanda with his back to me, kneeling on the ground of Juna's cave.

'Wanda?' I whispered. I stepped forward, looking over his shoulder, and saw a hawk clamped between his knees. He reached for a stone and held it up. 'No!' I cried, as he smashed the stone into the hawk's skull.

I was grabbed from behind, jolted from the vision.

'It's just me,' Zandi said, when I went to pull away. She guided me clear of the mist, then turned me to face her. 'You're shaking. What's wrong? What happened in there?'

'It's Wanda,' I said. 'I have to go to him.'

17. Suni

THE CLEAR LIGHT OF MORNING went some way to ease my fears. Dreamwalking wasn't possible while I was awake. Maybe Zandi was right, maybe I was just missing Wanda. I was eager to see him and deliver the monkey into his care.

Like all the keepers, Zandi had grown up with wild horses, able to call them from the herd. It was a black mare that carried us over the plains. For the most part, this side of the mountains was still desert; the rains that now fell had so far brought to life only sporadic oases in the otherwise lifeless sand.

Nature fared better close to the mountains. Thorn bushes, ferns and scrubby grasses had taken root in desert edging the range. On the slopes, thick scrubland sheltered predators and prey: mountains goats, hares and grey foxes among others. As we trekked the steep passes, I kept watch for mountain lions. They stood as tall as a man's waist, yet purred as softly as the cats around town. With teardrop markings on their faces, and black tufts of hair tipping their tails and ears, they were an extraordinary sight, but as always, I hoped not to see one: the skin of a such a lion fetched the highest price. In the days of the King, they had been the first of our wildlife hunted to extinction. I often thought they had returned with long memories of the past and felt glad they were elusive by nature.

We followed a well-worn path and arrived at the modern site of pilgrimage: a rocky outcrop overlooking a shallow escarpment. This had once been a levelled plateau at the entrance to the mines, and was where people came to remember those lost to the earthquakes. Looking out across the escarpment, we saw evidence of the landslide Patsy had spoken of, with the lower slopes buried in mounds of shale. It was an unsettling reminder of the power of the mountains.

After a night camping out on the flat summit, we crossed over into the valley. Riding across the grasslands, the sun was high in a clear blue sky, but as we neared Juna's cottage, traversing the hillocks on our approach, there was a change in the weather. It was too early in the season for rain, but thick grey clouds hung low over the cottage, as though a storm was brewing; clouds that oddly appeared nowhere else.

Rounding the hillside overlooking the cottage, I smiled to see the place that had once been home. There was still evidence of Juna's bachelor days, with a menagerie of wood carvings filling the ground to the side. Wanda's first attempt, a misshapen owl, was among them. Now, since becoming a family home, well-established crops occupied more of the plot.

Juna appeared in the doorway, as the horse slowed to a stop.

'Strange weather you've got here,' Zandi called out.

Juna didn't answer, just gave a slight nod. Usually we were welcomed with a warm greeting, but today he appeared oddly tense.

I dismounted, unstrapped the monkey's basket and rested it on my hip.

'See you at the forest in a few days,' I said, taking Zandi's hand and gently squeezing.

I lingered, watching her go as she kicked her heels and headed south. Then I turned and went to Juna.

Instead of his usual tight embrace, he received me with a loose, one-arm hug.

'Everything all right, Juna?' I asked, leaning back to look into his eyes. They were framed with dark circles as though he hadn't slept in days.

He nodded. 'It's good to see you.'

'You too.'

He turned to go inside, pausing as he looked at the basket under my arm.

'What've you got there, another orphan?' he asked.

I nodded. 'I think it's a tufted tamarin.'

I followed into the cottage, where Ntombi was sitting at the table. I went to her and kissed her cheeks.

'I would ask how you've been,' I said, resting the basket on the table and pulling out a chair. 'But you both look like you're not sleeping.' I sat down opposite Ntombi.

She reached across, patted my hand and said, 'We're fine.'

Seeing the brief, uncertain glance she shared with Juna, I wondered what they were hiding. I looked over at Luna kneeling by the fireplace. With her back to me, idly poking the crackling wood, she hadn't looked up since I'd arrived.

'Where's Wanda?' I asked.

'At the cave,' Juna said, with a tone that was oddly flat.

'Will you make us some tea, Juna,' Ntombi said. She turned towards the fireplace. 'Luna, come and say hello to Suni.'

Luna slowly stood and came to the table, eyes on the monkey's basket as she sat down.

'Hello, Luna,' I said.

She looked at me with a faint smile on her lips and a solemn look in her eyes. Unsettled by the tension in the room, I lifted the monkey out and held it against my chest.

'It's a tufted tamarin all right,' Juna said. He chopped up a paw paw and handed me a slice. 'It's young. I'd say you found it just in time.'

'It's going to need Wanda's help if it's to return to the forest,' I said, watching the monkey feed. I looked up expecting a response, but no one answered. I followed Juna's stray glance to the pile of bags packed in the corner. 'Will someone tell me what's going on? What are the bags for? Are you going somewhere?'

'We're moving to town,' Ntombi said. She met my eye briefly, before staring down at the table, her mouth set in a stubborn line.

I put a hand out to still Juna's arm, as he set the teapot on the table.

'Why?' I asked.

His gaze met mine but he didn't answer.

'Luna, go upstairs,' Ntombi said.

'Why?' Luna said, scowling at her mother.

'Because I said so,' Ntombi said. 'Do as you're told.'

Reluctantly, Luna left the table, dragging her feet as she climbed the ladder into the loft.

'Luna's ill,' Ntombi quietly said. 'We're going to stay with Juna's mother.'

'She doesn't look ill,' I said.

'She has terrible nightmares,' Ntombi said. 'She's even tried to run away; Juna found her all the way up in the mountains.'

I considered Patsy's version of events. If there was any truth to it, Luna's presence in town would cause chaos.

'Why would Luna run to the mountains?' I asked.

It was Juna who quietly answered, 'She might have been looking for Wanda.'

'More like she's scared of him,' Ntombi said, defiance in her eyes as she met Juna's gaze.

I looked from one to the other, confused by the tension. I had never known them argue before.

'Why would you say that?' I asked. 'What's happened?'

Ntombi's eyes glistened with tears as she said, 'There's something wrong with Wanda, something unnatural. The way he talks to animals, it's not right.'

I sat back in my chair. 'What are you talking about, Ntombi. Wanda's gifted. You know that.'

'I don't know whether it's a gift or a curse,' she said.

Her words stung. 'Since when did gifts become curses?'

'Ntombi doesn't mean it,' Juna said.

I kept my eyes fixed on Ntombi.

'I'm not talking about you,' she said. 'But there is something about Wanda. Luna says he's trying to control her and get inside her head. She says he's cursed with a shadow.' She rested her elbows on the table and leaned forward. 'Something's not right. We all heard it. My daughter needs help. I have to protect her.'

I shook my head. 'Whatever's upsetting Luna, I can't believe you're blaming Wanda.'

Ntombi didn't answer. She gripped her hands in front of her, staring down at the table with a cool resolute look on her face.

Her relationship with Wanda had always been difficult, but I never thought she would turn her back on him by choice. I turned to Juna, but he was heading for the door. I picked up the monkey and followed outside.

Juna was sitting on the bench, bent forwards with his head in his hands. I sat down next to him.

'I know what you're going to say,' he said, glancing at me before looking straight ahead. 'And you're right. But she won't listen. They had a terrible fight before Wanda left but I'm damned if I know what it's about. Neither one of them will tell me what it is between them.' He folded his arms and sat back. 'I think of Wanda like he's my own son, but Ntombi's always pushed him away. He pushes her away as well.' He turned to face me. 'But she is right about one thing. There's something wrong with Luna. I've never seen nightmares like she has. Even after she wakes up it's like she's gripped by some sort of madness, screaming about dragons!'

'Dragons?' I said, surprised to realise that Patsy hadn't been exaggerating after all. 'Where has Luna got ideas like that from?'

'You tell me,' Juna said. 'But wherever it comes from, Luna's screaming about burning in dragon fire!' He wiped a hand over his mouth. 'Ntombi blames Wanda, but he's the only one who can get through to Luna when she's like that. And when Wanda's not here, Luna gets worse.'

I rested a hand on his shoulder. 'You're not making any sense.'

'You can see it for yourself,' he said, looking up at the sky. 'This weather's not just strange; it's unnatural. It was after Wanda left that these storm clouds came. You won't see them anywhere else in the valley.'

I looked at the mass of grey cloud slowly rotating about a dark centre above the cottage. It was too early in the season for rain, and I had never seen storm clouds gather at single points. But it was surely just freak weather.

'What are you saying?' I asked.

'I'm saying that Luna's got some sort of power, power that's brought these storm clouds here. I know how it must sound, and don't ask me to explain it, but something's happening.' He paused, turning to face me. 'You remember in the palace, when we first saw the King, and that strange sound we all heard?' I nodded; none of us would ever forget. 'Well, I've heard it here, in the cottage.'

Juna had been there ten years ago, when together with the keepers we had invaded the palace and come face to face with King Rhonad. He was not the strong, fearsome leader I had expected, more of a creature than a man, rotten from the inside out from all the years possessed by the spirit of Orag. When he had spoken, Orag's voice had growled from his mouth, and when he moved there was the unexplainable sound of chirping, swarming insects.

'We both know Ntombi's wrong about Wanda,' he said. 'But I do think Luna would be better off in town. My mother's skilled in herbal lore, and she was at the palace for years. She knows what happened to the King as well as anyone. Maybe she'll know a way to help Luna.'

I put my hand on his arm and gently squeezed. 'I'm going to find Wanda.'

18. Wanda

MY LAST FLIGHT WITH THE hawk, feeding on raw flesh, had left me with the lingering temptation to taste fresh blood. Since then I had survived on berries and roots, afraid that hunting would weaken my resolve to give in to that temptation.

Whilst I fought against my own weakness, I feared Luna had given in to hers. Each day I looked out over the cottage from afar, watching swirling storm clouds overhead. Seeing Luna at the centre of the storm, I felt the bond between us. She needed me and I needed her. I needed to understand the bond between us, needed to find a way to stop us both from becoming more lost. But even Juna wouldn't let me near. And so each day, I turned my back on the storm and retreated to the cave with the shadow close at my back.

It was midday when I headed back across the grasslands from my viewpoint of the cottage. Spying tracks in the ground, I bent down low for a closer look. Seeing single lobed paw pads tipped with claw marks, followed by droppings of hair and bone fragments, I imagined the freedom of running wolves. It was days since I had had respite from the shadow, and I longed for it.

Further on, I found the hawk perched high in a lone red birch. I had nurtured many injured and orphaned creatures, cared for them until they were strong enough to be released. My first encounter with the hawk had been different. It had been just a youngling when I'd seen it fly over the cave, chased by an eagle. When I called out to it, it came to me, evading death. The cave had been at the centre of its territory ever since.

We had taken many flights together, but since I'd stayed for the kill, I hadn't seen the hawk. I sensed its distrust as it looked at me now from the high branch.

I had pushed my will too far, stayed for the kill, but surely the hawk couldn't know about my murderous dream. I was haunted by the sound of its skull cracking beneath the force of my own hand. I pushed the thought aside, gazing at its poised silhouette, imagining the air whistling through our flight feathers as we scanned the landscape. My heartbeat quickened, my mouth was watering, as my thoughts turned to the bloody scene of sharp talons and a hooked beak tearing flesh into bitesize pieces.

I swallowed, feeling excitement turn to confusion then shame as I locked eyes with the hawk. Hearing the shadow's swarming melody, feeling its cool touch closing in behind me, I clenched my teeth. I stared wide-eyed at the hawk, silently pleading with it to let me in. My heart sank when it turned away, spread its wings and flew off without me.

With shoulders slumped, I headed back to the cave.

My steps grew light when I saw smoke rising from the mouth of the cave. I hadn't expected to see Juna anytime soon. But when I climbed up over the ledge to the entrance, it was Suni I found crouched by the smouldering fire.

'I was wondering where you'd got to,' she said, welcoming me with open arms.

'I've missed you,' I said, hugging her back.

No matter what anyone thought of me, no matter what I thought of myself, Suni always looked at me in the same way. To her I was still a boy with a gift. I nestled my face into her shoulder, breathing in her musky odour, remembering the day she had rescued us both from the mines. I often wondered how life might have turned out if Ntombi had never showed up, and Juna had married Suni instead. But Suni preferred the company of women.

'Well, this is a nice welcome,' she said, leaning back to look at me. She brushed a loose strand of hair from my face and smiled. 'I've brought something with me.' She bent down, lifting a tamarin out of the basket at her feet. 'It was smuggled into town. It needs reintroducing back to the forest.'

I hesitated when she held it out to me, afraid it would sense in me what the hawk saw.

'Wanda?' Suni said.

I reached out a tentative hand, relieved to see the monkey grab my fingers. Warmed by its trust, I scooped it into my hands and held it against my chest. I smiled to feel the grip of its tiny fingers as it climbed up to sit on my shoulder.

Suni was watching me closely.

'He'll need to be accepted by a troop,' I said.

'So you can help?'

I nodded. 'Tamarins have big social groups. They're not difficult to track.'

She smiled and softly said, 'And you, Wanda. Are you all right?'

'I'm fine.'

Her eyes narrowed. 'You're too thin. You're not eating properly.' She picked a handful of mint leaves hanging from the roof, then dropped them into the pot of simmering water. 'Come, sit and eat. Juna packed us some supper.'

She unwrapped bread and cheese, laid it out on a flat stone, then ladled tea into two mugs. I tucked in, feeling my stomach growl at the sight of food.

Suni sat cradling her mug of tea and said, 'Did you know that Juna and Ntombi are leaving?' I dropped my hands into my lap and stared at her. 'They're taking Luna to live in town.' She paused then said, 'You didn't know.'

I shook my head.

'They're worried about Luna. They told me about the nightmares.'

'They want to take her away from me, don't they?' I quietly said.

'Is it no better between you and your aunt?'

'I think she hates me.'

'She doesn't hate you, Wanda.'

'She blames me for Luna.'

Suni paused, eyes clenched in frustration, then said, 'She's just worried about Luna. I know it's been difficult, but whatever's gone on, it's not your fault. Deep down, Ntombi knows that.'

I stared into space, afraid of what might happen if they took Luna away. Despite everything, she needed me and I needed her; I felt it in every bone of my body.

'You keep too much to yourself,' Suni said. I glanced at the shadow lurking close by, but quickly averted my eyes. 'I always hoped you and your aunt could put the past behind you, but you never have.'

'I've tried,' I said, meeting her gaze.

'I know she didn't always do right by you, Wanda, but she was so young when she took you in. It might help if you try to understand what life was like for her back then.' I stayed quiet to hide my frustration: I had heard it before. Suni reached over and put a hand on my knee. 'She was only fourteen when she took you in as a baby. There was no one to help her. She built that shack with her own hands and worked all hours to pay for it. She married Wiseman because she thought it might give you both an easier life. She didn't know he would beat her.'

'He beat us both,' I said, remembering the feel of the fire poker across my back. 'And she hit me, you know she did.'

'Yes, I know. And I know she regrets it. She regrets ever marrying that man.' She paused then said, 'You've both been hurt. Maybe it would help if we speak to your aunt together.'

When I didn't answer she looked away, staring down at the ground. Feeling the barrier between us, I was tempted to tell her my secrets, tempted to believe she might be able to help me. But I couldn't bear her knowing I wasn't the boy she thought I was.

Finally, I said, 'Talking wouldn't make any difference. She doesn't want me near Luna, that's all there is to it. But they shouldn't leave.'

'Why?'

I sighed, tired of the tension, the secrets and lies.

'You've been spending too much time on your own,' Suni said. 'Why don't you come and live with me and Zandi in town; you could make a new life for yourself.'

It was a tempting thought. Suni was like family, and she was gifted, but even she couldn't save me from the shadow. I felt the monkey's fingers gently tug at my hair. The infant's trust gave me hope that my connection with wildlife was not broken. That connection was the only thing that gave me respite from the shadow.

'My place is here,' I said.

19. Suni

I SUSPECTED THE GUARDED LOOK in Wanda's eyes was about more than a past he couldn't reconcile. Ever since his encounter with the Mantra, he often had a faraway look in his gaze that was too old for his years. He was gifted, but sometimes I wondered about the true cost of that gift.

But the next morning as we headed into the sacred forest, Wanda at ease with the tamarin perched on his shoulder, I was reminded of the boy I knew. He could name every species that made up the forest tapestry – all the trees, lizards, bats and birds – and chatted easily as we trekked the pathways. Even the monkey seemed to be listening, head cocked. Wanda came with me as far as the village clearing, home to a community of round mud huts. I had tried before to get him to visit Gogo, hoping she might see the secrets that burdened him, but Wanda would always find some excuse to refuse. Now, with the tamarin to take care of, I didn't press him. After agreeing to meet later, we parted ways.

I headed into the village, expecting the usual hive of activity. But walking the lanes between the huts, among goats, chickens and crops of corn and sugar cane, I saw no one. I hurried on, feeling uneasy: I had never seen it so quiet. Zandi was sitting in the doorway of her family home. There was a solemn look on her face as she came out to meet me.

'What is it?' I said. 'What's wrong? Where is everyone?'

She put her hands on my shoulders and gently said, 'Gogo's ill. They say she's dying. I'm so sorry, Suni.'

I stared at her in disbelief. Gogo was around a hundred years old, yet I had never imagined life without her. Wise woman of the forest, over the years she had grown central to the whole land. Her wisdom was relied upon; *I* relied on it to report back to the council. Moreover, she was my great grandmother, the only kin I had left aside from a ruined father.

I swallowed back the lump in my throat, and said, 'I have to go to her.'

Zandi nodded and gripped my hand as we set off through the narrow lanes.

Gogo's pending death commanded a respectful quiet that appeared to extend out into the trees, where even birdsong sounded dignified and understated. Arriving at the hut, I gently pushed the door open and went alone into the darkened room. Lit only by the faint glow of a smouldering fire, Gogo was curled on a grass mat, wrapped in a blanket, surrounded by the elders sitting cross-legged on the ground. She appeared frail, her skin ashen; I felt death was close.

'Gogo,' I quietly said.

Gogo slowly lifted her arm and reached her hand towards me. The elders didn't raise their heads when I stepped between them to kneel beside my great grandmother. I held her hand, gently kneading her soft sagging skin that felt cool.

'I knew you were coming,' she said, her voice quiet and croaking.

She glanced at the stones lying on the ground beside her. To my eyes it was just a random arrangement, but Gogo was a seer, skilled at revealing prophecies in the stones.

'Is there anything I can do for you,' I said, my eyes welling with tears. 'Are you comfortable?'

'Don't cry for an old woman.' Her voice was weak but stern. 'There's not much time. Tell me about the town. Is there still illness on the streets?'

Gogo never did have much time for sentiment. I took a deep breath to still my sadness, then said, 'Yes, and we still don't know how to cure it. Times are hard with farms suffering blight and people struggling to feed their families. Poaching is on the rise.' I paused, but Gogo squeezed my hand as though willing me to go on. 'I think we need the mist and keepers guarding the mountains. We've got no other way of stopping the poachers.'

She cleared her throat and said, 'No. We need to defend the shores. Darkness is coming.'

'But, Gogo, what darkness? We've seen pirates among the sea traders but nothing else. Our problems are here, on land. Wildlife is suffering; it's like history repeating itself.'

'What else,' she said, gazing into my eyes with a penetrating stare.

'I'm not sure. There was a landslide in the mountains a few days ago.'

'And the girl, Luna,' she said. 'Her name is written in the stones.'

I paused then said, 'I'm not sure about that either. Juna and Ntombi are worried about her. They say she has terrible nightmares and screams about dragons, as though she's got some sort of sickness of the mind.'

'Dragon,' Gogo whispered, closing her sagging eyelids. A moment later she looked back at me and said, 'A girl scarred by fire in the mountains, maybe there's a reason she's disturbed.'

'What do you mean?'

Gogo's eyes narrowed. 'You remember the legend I once told you: in ancient times a creature of darkness travelled in the eye of a storm, arriving here from distant lands. I've never known the spirit in the mountains called by the name, dragon.'

'It's just a child's imagination,' I said. After all I'd seen, I didn't deny the existence of a spirit in the mountains, but a dragon? Tales of flying serpents were legends brought by ships to our shores.

Gogo continued, regardless: 'When the storm hit, the mountains were reshaped, and the creature of darkness burrowed down deep into the mountain core.' Her voice grew soft until it was barely a whisper. I leaned in close, feeling the soft hairs on her chin as she continued. 'I always prayed that the grace of the Mantra could shield us from its evil, but I fear the dragon has a will of its own.' She paused, taking a long slow breath. 'I see the beginnings of a new weave. Darkness is coming from beyond our shores, but so too are our allies. The mountains…'

After another long pause I felt her shallow breath on my skin. Ear poised over her mouth, I waited for another breath, but none came.

'She's gone,' an old man quietly said, laying a hand on my shoulder.

I sat back and saw Gogo's staring eyes and open mouth. I placed a hand over her eyes, closing them for the final time.

GOGO'S BODY WAS PREPARED BY the elders: dressed in a cream burial gown, her hair wound into a bun, her wrists and ankles adorned with strings of beads, and a thin veil over her face. I led the procession that followed Gogo, as she was carried on her final journey to the sacred burial site. No amount of tears, no words of comfort, could fill the void Gogo left behind. For all the wisdom the elders held, there was no one to take the wise woman's place. Watching as she was lowered into the ground, I felt the loss like an empty well in my stomach. As the villagers held their hands up to the sky and raised their voices in a sombre funeral chant, I stared straight ahead, fearing what was to come. Our land was under threat, and I knew nothing more than vague prophecies that left the face of the enemy undetermined. Our people were fractured, and the only person with any hope of steering us through was gone.

20. Wanda

AT THE FOREST EDGE, I waved Suni and Zandi off as they started their journey home on horseback. For my part it was a reluctant goodbye: I was nervous of the thought of being left alone. I reached up to stroke the monkey perched on my shoulder, reassured by its presence. As I headed back into the trees in search of a troop, I wondered if a good deed could overshadow my haunting dream of the hawk.

Mournful cries carried through the canopy: prayers sung for the wise woman's passing. It sounded like a uniform, low-pitched hum, unlike the chorus of birdsong. I tried identifying the birds, but it was a confusing melody. I had grown used to the way the shadow distorted shades and notes, but in the forest, filled with competing colours and sounds, identifying individual species proved difficult. Suni's company had reminded me of the boy I'd once been, a life I wanted back. So, I strained to hear, to distinguish notes that had once been familiar, but was left just feeling frustrated.

When the chill of the shadow moved in closer, the monkey gripped tighter to my neck. Whether it was a coincidence or because it sensed my shadow, I couldn't be sure: its innocent chatter was little more than baby talk. Still, I quickened my pace, trying different paths until I spotted some interesting signs. Chunks of pomelo fruit peel littered the ground, with small indented teeth marks in the hard, sour peel. There was more scattered further down the path, and tamarin droppings in among fallen leaves. Following the trail, I heard low-pitched clacking calls signifying a troop gathered for familial preening. I cupped a protective hand around the monkey clinging to my neck, wondering how much it remembered of its own kind. Introducing this baby would be a delicate task, with no guarantee it would be accepted; a rejected infant would be killed by an adult male.

Hearing high-pitched screeching in the trees, I looked up to see the troop's leader giving out the warning call. I lifted the monkey down from my shoulder, held it close to my chest, and slowly stepped back into the undergrowth. Noticing movement ahead in the trees, I saw the troop of tufted tamarins in the branches. Keeping my head low, I moved back further, until the warning cries stopped. Away from the guarding male, I rounded on the troop from another side, spotting several adolescents grouped together on a low branch. I crept closer, gently placing the baby onto the branch close to the youngsters and stepped back. A young female was watching as I sank back into the bush. I watched, still and silent, as she crept along the branch to the baby, head cocked as it let out a soft whimpering cry. She sat down next to it for a moment, before taking the baby's arm and swinging it round to sit on her back. One by one the youngsters accepted the orphan, teaching it the art of preening which it practised with clumsy fingers. When an adult female came and gave fruit to the orphan, I left. Her swollen belly told me she was the breeding matriarch, with authority to see the baby accepted by the whole troop.

I sprang two traps along the path on my way back through the forest. It was a savage way for a monkey to die, left hanging by a hand or foot, slowly starving to death, cut down and skinned by a poacher; it was most likely how the orphan's mother had died. A few had been rescued but they were destined to live out their days with a missing limb. Further on, I heard a pitiful call that led to a mound of freshly-dug earth. Next to it was a hole, concealed by a thin layer of mesh stuck with leaves that had been broken through. I peered into the hole, so deep it looked to be shoulder height. Trapped at the bottom was a long-eared fox, crumpled into a twisted position as though its back was broken. It would die soon, but not soon enough, judging by its agonising cries. I swung my legs over and climbed in.

The fox looked at me with fear in its eyes as I knelt beside it. With no weapon to hand, I clamped my hands around its snout and held tight as it squirmed. I considered trying to offer words of comfort, but I just wanted it over. Finally, it stopped twitching and lay dead on the ground. I slumped down next to it and rubbed my hands over my eyes, consumed by the smell of death and the cold of the shadow. A vision flashed behind my closed eyes: the fox lunged at my face with eyes shining and teeth bared in a snarl. I sat back, startled, and looked at the fox. It was just a corpse.

I climbed out, hurriedly scooping earth in to fill the hole, determined at least that no more creatures would die here. I wiped a hand over my sweat-covered brow and paused, sensing the change: this wasn't my usual cold sweat. I looked up, squinting in the bright sun dappling through the branches. Feeling the warmth of the sun on my face, I looked down at my hands and arms and saw the rich brown tones of my skin. Confused by the sudden clarity of my senses, I looked at the shadow that was slowly drifting away from me. As the distance between us grew, I savoured the colours of the forest, daring to think that the curse was somehow lifting. Seeing the forest untainted by the shadow, I felt lighter than I had done in years. And when I saw what was standing behind me, I stopped and stared in wonder.

The Mantra, as tall as the trees, had the body of a deer, legs tipped with yellow two-toed hooves, and a long neck lined with a soft mane. It wore the face of every creature. Now, the eyes of an owl looked out towards the shadow. When it turned its gaze on me, its features transformed into a bat. And when it reached down with its long neck, the eyes of a fox gazed upon me.

I looked into the deep pools of its eyes, hopeful for salvation. The Mantra had put its trust in me before, now I could only hope it saw the same boy. It closed its eyes and inhaled a long slow breath, as though smelling me. When it raised its head and exhaled, its muzzle transformed into the snout of a boar. Once it was standing tall, it was the face of a monkey looking down at me.

Seeing the bristles of red hair on its chin, the white markings below its eyes that were framed with long black lashes, I said in its tongue, 'Help me.'

But the Mantra stepped back and turned, heading away into the trees. I stared after its tracks, eyes and ears fixed on the bright colours and clear sounds of the forest. But when the cool of the shadow closed in behind me, my view was cast in its familiar shade. Rejected by the Mantra, I ran from the forest, the scent of death lingering on my hands.

21. Luna

I WAS IN THE FOREST, at the edge of the clearing, listening to the sound of children's laughter in the trees. It grew louder as running footsteps headed in my direction. Two children appeared from out of the trees; it was Wanda and me, both younger. I looked about five years old. They didn't see me as they ran past, chasing one another across the clearing and into the trees on the far side.

I listened to their laughter slowly fade, and looked down at my hands and arms. I was the ghostly form of my ten-year-old self. The silent part of me had never appeared in the dream before, and where was the girl?

She appeared soon after, furtive as she crept into the shade of a nearby elderbirch. There was fear on her face as she huddled against the tree trunk, looking up at the sky over the clearing.

I reached up to touch my chest, remembering the sight of my ribs cracking, but I had no physical form. The silent part saw all, and yet my memories felt confused. I watched the girl tightly clutching her shawl, while her other hand mindlessly rubbed her belly. I wondered whether fire was warming her insides as she watched in fearful anticipation of the dragon.

A spotted flycatcher landed on the bough of a nearby tree, calling for its mate with the familiar succession of long, high-pitched calls. The calls gradually dipped to a strangely low note, before the flycatcher flew off, disappearing into the canopy. I glanced back at the branch it had perched on, realising that something was different: the bark was covered in pale grey lichen that was slowly creeping down the tree and into the surrounding undergrowth. The purple colour of ground-covering sweet violets had paled to pink, birdsong faded from the canopy leaving the forest eerily quiet, and the light grew dim. The girl didn't seem to notice the surrounding changes, as she crouched low to the ground, eyes fixed on the sky.

Leaves rustled in the treetops, fanned by the dragon's beating wings as its pale grey underbelly flew overhead, circling the area. It was only a matter of time before the beast found the girl. I wanted to call out, to tell the girl to run, but the silent part of me had no voice. I went to her and reached out to touch her, meaning to return to the physical body. But nothing happened. I remained detached from the whole. I bent down and stared into the girl's eyes, but she didn't see me. She was lost, caught in the dragon's sights, and I was helpless to save her. I was helpless to save myself.

Hearing children's laughter from behind, I turned to look. I was surprised to see the white woman with flaming orange hair looking back at me. As before, she appeared as a ghost, watching from behind a nearby tree with curiosity in her eyes. She stayed for a moment, until the laughter grew near. Then she turned her back and walked away, as dappling sunlight filtered down.

My five-year-old self arrived with Wanda, laughing as they chased each other through the trees. Overhead, the spotted flycatcher landed on a branch, singing for its mate. I smiled to see the colourful plumage, then looked back down at the girl. But she was gone, along with the shadow of the dragon's flight.

22. Suni

I WAS RELUCTANT TO LEAVE Wanda alone in the valley, but he wouldn't leave, and I was needed in town. Besides, as Zandi reminded me, Wanda was a man now, capable of taking care of himself. The same could not be said of the town; worried over how Luna would be received, we rode the horse hard.

On the journey home I pondered over Gogo's parting words but could find no sense in them. Dragons were surely just myth, but even if I tried to imagine one buried in the mountains, Gogo's own logic made no sense. Why insist on guarding the shores against encroaching darkness, if we had a dragon to contend with? What exactly were we supposed to be guarding against, and who were our allies from beyond the shores? I didn't dare mention dragons to Zandi, knowing she would only mock the very idea.

It was the middle of the night when we arrived home, stiff and tired after a long ride. We headed down the cellar steps to bed, but were stopped by a loud banging at the door.

'Who on earth's that at this time?' Zandi said, turning around and handing me the candle.

I led the way back up the steps, opened the door, and was surprised to find Sunette out on the street, wearing just her nightgown. There was fear in her wide eyes as she held onto her sides, breathing heavily as though she had been running.

'Sunette, what are you doing here at this time?' I said.

'You've got to come quickly. It's Luna.'

'Is she having a nightmare?' I asked, grabbing a shawl from the hook on the wall.

'It's no nightmare,' Sunette said. 'Come on, both of you, hurry.'

She led us at a run down the street.

Approaching Sunette's house, we slowed to a cautious walk. The shutters and front door were rattling in their hinges; and strange sounds were coming from inside, banging, thudding and scraping, like furniture being dragged across the floor.

'What's going on in there?' I said, looking back to see Sunette had stopped away from the house. She didn't answer, just wrapped her arms around her middle.

Zandi reached for the door handle. Her hand shook with the force of the door rattling as she lifted the latch and pushed. But the door didn't open. She leaned in with her shoulder and shoved, but it still didn't budge. I raised my hand, intending to thump it against the door, but paused, hand poised mid-air. The door had stopped rattling, the shutters were still, and disturbances from inside the house had grown quiet. I tried the latch, and this time it opened.

Inside, the room was in chaos, with chairs knocked over and broken pots strewn across the floor. Juna was standing with his back pinned against the wall, across the room from where Ntombi was sitting on the bed, her face streaked with tears. Both were staring at Luna who sat cross-legged in the corner, her head lowered, hair hanging down over her face. There was a strange sound coming from her corner, distant at first but growing louder: clicking, humming and screeching like swarming insects. I recognised the eerie sound and saw that Zandi did too.

I turned to Luna and walked slowly towards her, pausing when she raised her head, her eyes meeting mine with a cold stare.

'Stay back,' she said, in a deep growling voice.

It was Orag speaking through her, the same voice once heard from the mouth of the King. I stopped and held my breath not knowing what to expect. She flung her head back and began knocking it hard against the wall. A strange breeze stirred. The door slammed shut, the shutters started rattling again, and furniture rocked, wood knocking against the stone floor. Juna side-stepped as the table slid across the floor in his direction, slamming into the wall where he had stood a moment ago. The head banging suddenly stopped as Luna sat forward, fixing Juna in a hard stare.

'The dragon is coming,' she said in the same rough voice. 'You will all burn in its fire.'

The hum of screeching and clicking grew louder, the breeze inside the cottage blew stronger, and Ntombi clung to the covers as the bed started shaking. Zandi ran to Luna and slapped her across the face. Luna lashed out, spitting and snarling, clawing at Zandi's face. I ran to help, and together with Juna we grappled with Luna's flaying arms. She was a ten-year-old girl with the strength of a grown man. Finally, her head flopped forwards. Pinning her arms at her sides, we felt her body slowly relax.

The room fell still. When Luna finally raised her head, I saw the face of a frightened child.

'It's burning,' she cried, in her own pitiful voice, holding a hand to her cheek where the scar was red and inflamed.

I helped her to her feet and took her to her mother.

THE NEXT MORNING, I SAT with Zandi and Juna at the table in the backyard. Sunette brought out a tray of coffee, leaving Ntombi and Luna still sleeping inside. Next door, Anita was watching from the window. When she saw me looking, she scowled then moved out of sight. With the houses built so close together, she was sure to have heard the night's events. Since Anita traded at market, the whole town would soon be talking about Luna.

I took a mug and sipped the coffee, savouring the flavour of cinnamon. Juna dragged on his pipe and exhaled a huge cloud of smoke.

'Luna's nightmares have been getting worse,' he said, restlessly tapping the pipe against the table. 'But I've never seen one as bad as that.'

'That was no nightmare,' I said.

'No it wasn't,' Sunette added. 'The spirit of Orag was with us last night.'

'We have to help her,' Juna said, staring at his mother, but she dropped her gaze, looking down at the table.

She was shaking her head when she looked back at him. 'I'm sorry son. I wish I could help but I don't know how. You shouldn't have brought her here, it's too dangerous. If the townspeople find out, they'll come for her.'

Juna leaned back and brushed his hands through his hair. 'Ntombi won't go back. She's got it into her head that somehow this is all Wanda's influence. It's why we came: she wanted to get Luna away from him.'

I put a hand on Sunette's arm and said, 'I think it's better if Luna does stay here. We'll sort something out, and at least this way we can all keep an eye on her.'

Ntombi and Luna appeared in the doorway. There was an anxious look in Ntombi's tired eyes as she walked towards us, one arm leaning heavily on her walking stick, Luna clutching the other. As they joined us at the table, Luna seemed to be her usual self, appearing relaxed as though oblivious of the night's possession.

'Are you feeling better this morning, Luna?' I asked.

Ntombi cast me a wary look but Luna just nodded, frowning as though confused.

'I'm glad,' I said. I poured a cup of milk and handed it to her. 'Do you remember last night?'

She shook her head.

'You don't remember having a nightmare?' I said. 'You spoke about a dragon.'

Luna looked at her mother. 'I don't understand. Why is everyone upset?'

Ntombi shook her head and forced a smile. 'We're not upset.'

'I want to go home,' Luna said. 'I want to see Wanda.'

'I know,' Ntombi said, 'but we need to stay here for a while.'

The frown on Luna's face turned into a scowl as she stood up. Ntombi reached for her hand, but Luna brushed her mother aside, turning to face the house. When she turned back round, dark eyes rested on Ntombi.

Luna's lips parted but it was Orag's growling voice that spoke: 'Is it true my real father was a bastard?'

There was a moment of strained silence, before Luna turned away and walked with shuffling steps back into the house.

Ntombi held her face in her hands. Juna put a comforting hand on her shoulder, but there was a helpless look on his face as he stared at me. I left them there and went with Zandi, following Luna into the house. Keeping a safe distance, we found her standing in the far corner, quietly facing the wall. Movement glimpsed through the open window caught our attention.

'Now what do we do?' Zandi whispered, looking out at the gathering crowd. Anita stood, at the front.

'I'll go talk to them,' I said.

I glanced nervously at Luna but she hadn't moved. I opened the door ajar and slipped outside, followed by Zandi.

Anita stepped forward. 'You're hiding a witch in there.'

'What have you been saying, Anita?' I said. 'What are you all doing here?'

'The girl brought evil to that house last night,' Anita said. 'I thought I might be killed in my own bed.'

Vikki pushed her way through to the front and yelled, 'There she is. That's the girl I saw in the mountains, screaming about a dragon!'

I turned and saw Luna standing in the doorway, her hair blowing in a sudden breeze. As she came out to face the crowd, the scar on her cheek glowed, an orange light shining out through the cracks.

'Luna, come back inside,' Juna said, appearing behind her.

Luna turned to face him, head cocked as she spoke in the growling voice, 'You don't control me.'

She held an arm out towards him. There was no physical contact, but by her gesture alone, Juna was flung back into the house. Luna slowly turned to face the crowd, raising her arms out at her sides. A gusting wind blew all around.

'The good gifts can't save you,' she growled. 'You will all burn in dragon fire!'

Shocked faces watched as a bolt of lightning flashed in the sky above her. With arms splayed and head tilted back, Luna rose from the ground, hanging mid-air.

The crowd fled.

23. Suni

STORM CLOUDS HUNG PERMANENTLY ABOVE Sunette's house and a strange wind blew through the surrounding streets. When Luna's anger riled, lightning streaked the dark sky. During fits of rage, she moved objects with her mind, using them as weapons against anyone who tried to get close. And through it all, cracks of orange light shone through the lines of her scar as she threatened the coming of a dragon. Sunette's neighbours all abandoned their homes; soon no one would come near the street where 'the mad girl' lived.

I spoke with everyone I knew skilled in herbal lore, but between us we had no knowledge that could counteract an apparent possession. Juna was convinced that Wanda could help and suggested sending for him, but Ntombi refused. Whether or not Wanda might see what the rest of us could not, I was glad he was safely away from the presence of Orag. And so we were forced to watch, helpless, as Luna lost her appetite. In the times she was calm she would stay close by her mother's side, appearing like a confused, frightened girl. But even Ntombi was furtive around her own daughter.

Gripped by this nightmare, rumour quickly turned to fact. Soon Luna's 'madness' was said to be infectious, responsible for the blight, apparent quakes in the mountains, and the outcasts' affliction. The valley beyond the mountains was commonly referred to as 'witch' valley, and the mist with its guard of keepers was said to be haunted; an unnatural barrier to keep the darkness in.

The town was more fractured than it had ever been. I felt the undercurrent of danger, feared the townspeople would rise up against us as they had done when I was a girl. With Luna's powers evident in the storm clouds, threats were kept at bay. But for how long? With no resolution to the crisis, I retreated to the shores of the estuary, desperately putting all my hopes on Gogo's parting words, of allies from beyond our shores.

Ships came and went but I saw nothing that inspired hope. Until, one day, the strangers arrived.

It was midday when Zandi and I watched a long boat break free from the anchored ship and steadily row to shore. The men at the oars appeared nothing out of the ordinary, but two men and a woman sitting at the helm were different. They looked to be in their middle years, with skin as white as chalk and clothes grander than any merchant we'd seen before. The men wore tailored tunics and trousers, and the woman's emerald green dress had detailed embroidery fashioned around the front that glittered like gold. I gazed at her long orange hair cascading down her back; I didn't know there was such a thing as hair the colour of fire.

The unusual colouring and apparent wealth of the strangers proved to be a spectacle, as a crowd gathered on the riverbank where the long boat moored. The three strangers stepped out onto land, led by one of the men who approached the onlookers with confidence in his stride. He glanced up at the eastern skies, where the storm hung low over the town, then turned to address the crowd.

'We've heard about the girl, Luna, and the troubles you face. We've come to offer our help.'

'Who are you?' one woman asked.

'My name is Brahim Rayne Yangsen. This is my sister, Adela, and my brother, Ray. Is there a leader among you I can speak with? There isn't much time.'

One by one, faces turned towards where I stood with Zandi. The Rayne Yangsens came to us, each of them initiating shaking mine and Zandi's hand. I felt awkward by the formality, and the piercing stare of their blue eyes.

'What do you know about Luna?' I asked.

83

'It's common knowledge on the seas,' Brahim said. 'By the grace of the temple, it looks like we've arrived just in time.' He cleared his throat then said, 'Forgive me. I haven't asked for your introductions.'

'My name is Suni and this is Zandi.'

Brahim raised his eyebrows as though expecting me to continue. Adela stepped forward and put a hand on her brother's arm.

'There's not much time,' she said, resting her gaze on me. 'We must speak with your people. This land is facing an evil beyond what you can imagine. If the dragon is unleashed, the whole world will be under threat.'

'Dragon!' Zandi said. 'You sound like Luna.'

'The good gifts will keep us safe,' Brahim said.

'What does that mean?' I asked.

'I understand you have many questions. But like my sister said, we *must* address your people.'

Zandi said, 'If you start talking about dragons to the townspeople, you'll make things worse than they already are.'

'May the skies be merciful,' Brahim said. 'But without our help, things *will* get worse, much worse.'

A MEETING WAS CALLED IN the old school hall. The Rayne Yangsens sat among council members at the front. I took my seat between Adela and Zandi, and looked out into the audience, as they pleaded for help.

'Where do you come from?'

'Can you save us?'

'Why is this happening?'

Already our guests were being looked upon as saviours.

Sunette repeatedly hit the gavel, until the room fell quiet. Then Brahim stood up to address the townspeople.

'We come from the islands of the far western archipelago. My homeland understands the troubles you face all too well. As religious scholars from the islands' ancient temple, my family are well versed in the power of the dragons.'

His words were met with sombre silence, until more people called out.

'The mad girl's a witch,' Anita said. 'She brings lightning out of the sky. She'll kill us all.'

'She caused an earthquake in the mountains,' Patsy added.

Brahim turned to Patsy and said, 'Tell me about the mountains.'

'I was there with my daughter,' she said. 'We were almost killed in the landslide. It's just as it was ten years ago, when earthquakes killed our men in the mines.'

'Luna was only a baby then,' Sunette said, adding reason to the argument. She turned to Brahim, 'That was at the time of King Rhonad's death. He was a man reduced to madness, possessed by the spirit of Orag.'

Brahim glanced at Adela and Ray. Their confident poise seemed shaken as they shared a silent exchange.

'What are we talking about the King for?' Anita said. 'It's Luna we should be talking about. *She's* the one threatening us with a dragon!'

As more angry voices shouted out, Brahim gestured with his hands for quiet.

'Understand this,' he said, 'Luna has been chosen by the dragon, but she is not your enemy.'

'This is nonsense,' Zandi said. 'Dragons are nothing more than myth.'

Brahim raised an eyebrow as he looked at her. 'Where we come from, no one would doubt the existence of dragons. Our people have lived in the shadow of the Dragon Lands for centuries.'

'Have you seen a dragon?' Zandi asked, scepticism plain to see on her face.

Brahim said, 'It is long since dragons ruled the sky, but they are no mere legend. My homeland was forged from the history of the dragons.'

'I don't see what the history of your homeland has got to do with us,' Zandi said.

'No witch from the valley speaks for us,' Anita said. 'We want to hear what he has to say.'

I put my hand on Zandi's and gently squeezed.

'The history of the islands is relevant to all corners of the world, none more so than here,' Brahim said. He sipped from a cup of water then continued. 'Four ancient dragons lie sleeping on the Dragon Lands, watched over by the temple. As warders of the temple, we have the power to keep the dragons from waking. No one knows the reason, but one dragon fled the islands during the war. It is here, in your mountains, sleeping under the power of the warders.'

'Is it possible?' Sunette quietly said. 'A dragon in the mountains?'

'I think it might be,' I said, leaning forward to rest on my elbows. I looked up at Brahim. 'My great grandmother, a wise woman, told a story from ancient times, of a creature of darkness travelling in the eye of a storm. The story tells that it arrived here from distant lands and burrowed deep down in the mountain.'

'Then you know what I say is true,' Brahim said.

'Even if it is,' Zandi said. 'I don't see what this has to do with Luna.'

Brahim addressed the audience. 'Luna possesses the power of a warder. It is a gift that can protect you all from the dragon, but, untrained, that same gift will lead Luna down the path of madness. She can learn to channel her energy to keep the dragon from waking, or else fall prey to the dragon's mind.'

'What can we do?' I asked.

'Bring the girl to us,' Brahim said. 'Here, in this place, we will begin her training.'

24. Suni

'ARE YOU SURE ABOUT THIS?' Juna said, when I delivered the news that we must hand Luna over. 'We don't know these people. How can we can trust them?'

'I know it's hard,' I said. 'But what choice do we have?'

'None,' Ntombi said, staring down at Luna sound asleep on the bed. It had taken hot milk laced with three draughts of sleeping potion for her to fall asleep. 'For so long, I tried to deny it. I blamed Wanda. But my daughter has powers even I'm afraid of.' She wiped a tear from her eye and looked at Juna. 'I had resigned myself to the fact that evil had taken her, but if what these strangers say is true, our daughter is the one who can protect us all. Now there is hope.'

WE LAID LUNA IN THE back of the cart beside Ntombi, and led the mule through the streets, watched from afar by the braver onlookers. Approaching the school, we were forced to push our way through a crowd of outcasts all gathered outside. It was Ray who opened the gate for us. While we went into the yard where Brahim and Adela were waiting, Ray joined the outcasts out on the street, clutching a knapsack over his shoulder as he closed the gate behind him.

'If the outcasts are causing you any trouble,' I said, 'I can get the keepers to move them on.'

'It's no trouble,' Brahim said. 'Ray is used to administering to the sick.'

'Do you know what's wrong with the men?' I asked.

'That's what Ray is trying to find out,' Brahim said. 'He will do what he can. The men need care, not exile. Dragons gain power feeding on lost souls.'

When the gate opened and Ray came back in, I caught a glimpse of the street and was surprised to see the outcasts had all dispersed without a fuss.

Overhead, thick grey clouds moved in, eclipsing the sun. As Luna stirred, Brahim climbed in next to her with a coil of rope.

He paused, looked at Ntombi and said, 'We have to bind her hands and feet, for her own safety and ours.'

Ntombi nodded.

Just as Brahim finished tying Luna's ankles together, she opened her eyes. Still groggy, she fumbled with her bound hands.

'Try to relax, Luna,' Juna said, reaching into the cart to put a hand on her shoulder. 'We're all here to help you get well.'

'Mother!' Luna cried.

'These people can help you,' Ntombi said. Her voice was firm but there were tears in her eyes.

'What are you doing?' Luna cried, kicking against the cart. 'Take me home. I want to go home!'

'We can all go home, when you're well,' Juna said.

Luna struggled and cried as Brahim and Ray lifted her out of the cart and sat her on a chair by the tree. Rope was wrapped around her middle, tying her to the trunk. Once secured, she appeared to calm. Her shoulders relaxed, her head flopped forwards, hair hanging down over her face as she fell quiet. A moment later, a long low growl started. Luna slowly raised her head, orange light shining out from the lines of her scar as she stared into space. Then she started spitting and gnashing her teeth like a caged animal.

'You should go,' Brahim said.

As we turned to leave, a bolt of white lightning lit the sky.

FROM BEYOND THE SCHOOL GATES, we watched and waited for signs of Luna's improvement, but each day the storm worsened until dark clouds hung low over the whole town. With the eye of the storm swirling over the school, and bolts of lightning randomly scorching the sky, the town prayed for a miracle.

While the storm showed no signs of abating, there was unexpected good fortune to be found with the outcasts. Theirs was a remarkable transformation as they regained their desire for food, and began washing daily, taking pride in their appearance. Fights decreased and they stopped scratching, allowing the sores on their skin to heal. Seeing Ray counselling them through their recovery gave credence to the Rayne Yangsen's claims of authority, despite the fact the storm still raged.

One evening, from across the street, I looked out at the group of outcasts congregating by the school gates. I hadn't seen my father since before the storm and was curious to see whether his health had also improved. My eyes rested on his face. Seeing his skin clear of open wounds, his appearance clean and tidy, he seemed to have recovered. He was looking in my direction as I crossed the street towards him, but up close his eyes looked beyond me, glazed and vacant. I was standing right in front of him but he gave no acknowledgement.

'What's wrong with you?' I said. 'Don't you want to see me? You act like you couldn't care less that I'm your daughter.'

His eyes met mine only briefly before he looked away.

Ray was there among the men. 'Don't worry yourself,' he said, coming to stand beside me. 'It's just the medication. Give him time.'

'What medication are you giving them?' I asked. 'What's wrong with him?'

'Not here.' He put his hand on my shoulder, guiding me away down the street. 'The outcasts, as you call them, have suffered sickness of the mind. Once they were somebody, respected, with purpose, until they were nobody. Cast out of society. Exiled. Hated.'

I stopped, turning to face him. 'Whatever you think you know, whatever they've told you, you're not from here. You don't know what some of those men did.'

'I'm not here to defend what they did or didn't do in the past,' he said. 'Maybe they did wrong, but they had purpose to their day and that gave them self-respect. When they lost that, they lost hope. The mind and body work together; when the mind loses the will, the body becomes sick.'

'So what are you treating them with?' I asked.

'A rare herb grown on the islands. We've seen this illness before and know how to treat it. We'll get your father well, but you need to give him time. Right now, seeing you won't help his recovery.'

I TRIED AGAIN TO UNCOVER the mystery, but each time I received the same vague account of an illness treated with herbs I could never see, or smell, or handle. Now and again I witnessed small packages being handed about, but Ray had a persuasive nature, able to bring my questions to an end while keeping me at a distance. While Brahim and Adela remained behind the school gates with Luna, each day Ray would come out to 'minister' to the outcasts. And as their health appeared to improve, so too did the bonds between them. Not long ago they had scrapped worse than cats and dogs; now they appeared as close as brothers.

25. Suni

THE STORM CONTINUED AND NTOMBI grew restless for news of her daughter. But she was forbidden from entering the gates, told by Adela that they were working to strengthen Luna's mind against the will of the dragon; sight of her mother would only jeopardise the progress they had made. I tried in vain to comfort Ntombi, but I couldn't even reassure myself. Beneath a dark sky, the atmosphere throughout town was thick with fear. As normal life came to a standstill, I felt hope slipping away.

Each morning I walked out to the estuary with Zandi, gazing out over the seascape topped with clear blue skies. We were suffering the storm at a time that should be the start of summer and I longed to feel hot sun on my skin. One day we were greeted by a welcome sight: the raft people had arrived. This floating community of interlinked platforms, anchored just off the shore, was so sprawling in size it appeared like a town on water, sturdy despite the drifting tides. It was home to a hundred or more nomadic sea folk, who arrived each summer to trade. One of the raft people, Nisrin, had been my mother's good friend. She had looked after Mata when she was sick, and arranged for my passage on the rafts when I had needed it ten years ago.

I looked out beyond the surf, watching and waiting. I longed to see Nisrin and feel the warmth of her easy smile, but lately the storm had been turning sailors away. When a single canoe finally broke free of the floating community, I squeezed Zandi's hand. A slow smile spread across my face as I recognised the lone figure paddling to shore. Seeing the strength of Nisrin's strokes as she glided through the water, her thick yellow hair and weather-beaten skin bronzed from a life at sea, it was reassuring to think that some things hadn't changed. I waded with Zandi into the water and pulled the boat up onto the shore.

'How are my two favourite land dwellers?' Nisrin said, accepting my hand as I helped her out of the canoe.

'Happy to see you,' I said.

She kissed mine then Zandi's cheek and put her arms over our shoulders.

'This place is the talk of the seas,' she said, looking out over the town. 'You must have had this storm for weeks. No one else will come in from the rafts.' She looked at me. 'Is it true what I've heard, about Luna.'

'That depends what you've heard,' I said. 'But it might well be.'

I tilted my head to rest on her shoulder, breathing in the smell of sea salt lingering in her hair.

'Well that sounds ominous,' Nisrin said. 'And probably best talked about over tea.'

We took Nisrin home and soon had a fire going in the hearth. Over a pot of mint tea laced with sugar, we told of the events leading up to the storm. Nisrin had never been to the valley or met Juna, Ntombi, Luna or Wanda, but I had told her about them over the years. She quietly listened without judgement: raft people were known for believing in the spirits of the land and sea. After telling about the Rayne Yangsens claims of training Luna as a warder, Nisrin turned away, gazing into the flames.

'What is it?' I asked.

There was a thoughtful pause before she looked at me and said, 'I know the place you're talking about. The history of the islands is well known on the rafts. Five islands named after five mages who once ruled the archipelago: Raven, Drake, Brennus, Albin and Evren.'

'Evren?' I said, glancing at Zandi.

'We've heard that name before,' Zandi said, 'from a sailor. He said this town was turning into the next rat-infested port of Evren.'

'We didn't know what he meant,' I added.

'The island of Evren used to be the main port of trade,' Nisrin said. 'But the rafts haven't been there for years. The docks turned into a crime-ridden place, hardly like here, although…' She paused, looking over at the window.

'What is it?' Zandi asked.

'This storm reminds me of the islands,' Nisrin said, sitting forward in her chair as she turned to face us. 'The stories go that the mages became so consumed by their desire for more power, they in turn were consumed. They lost their human forms and transformed into dragons. Their breath turned to fire and their wings carried them to war in the skies. The Great War almost destroyed the island chain.' She reached for her mug and cupped it in her hands. 'One island is still a barren wasteland and is said to be where the dragons fell. They call it the Dragon Lands.'

'Brahim mentioned that place,' I said.

'The rafts won't go near,' Nisrin said. 'There's a permanent storm over the Dragon Lands said to carry a song in its winds, an enchantment that lures sailors overboard to drown in the sea.'

'And what about the temple of warders?' I asked.

Nisrin sipped her tea then said, 'It's told that the mages had been too greedy for power. The creatures they had become were so big, they couldn't consume enough to sustain themselves. To survive they began hibernating, and that was when their weakness was found. There were those who possessed gifts from the time of the mages.'

'Warders?' I asked.

Nisrin nodded.

Zandi sat back in her chair. 'All this talk of dragons, how do we even know it's true?'

'We don't,' Nisrin said. 'No one alive has seen a dragon, but the stories survive, and warders believe them enough to dedicate their lives to their religion.' She put her mug down, gently shaking her head as she stared at the table. 'You say the Rayne Yangsens are from the temple, but it just doesn't make sense.' She paused, looking back at us. 'Warders also call themselves priests and priestesses. They're a people shrouded in mystery, dedicated only to their religion. Some say they are centuries old, sharing a long life-bond with the dragons they ward for, using their power to keep the dragons from waking. They live a humble existence with no desire for comfort or wealth. They want only to serve and keep peace in the world. And they don't leave the temple walls.'

'Well that sounds nothing like the Rayne Yangsens,' Zandi said. 'Do you think they're not who they say they are?'

Nisrin shrugged a little, and tilted her head.

'We know they have knowledge of healing,' I said. 'They've been treating the outcasts.' I never mentioned my father in Nisrin's company, in case she thought I was betraying my mother's memory.

'And are the outcasts getting better?' Nisrin asked.

'They seem to be.'

Nisrin gently shook her head. 'Warders spend their days in ritual and prayer, they don't travel to distant lands and tend to the sick. They say Luna is a warder, but stories I've heard say an untrained warder is only susceptible to madness of their own minds; they don't have the kind of power that can create a storm.'

I stood up and went to the fire, idly poking the coals. 'We handed Luna to people we don't know.' I turned to look back at Nisrin. 'We didn't know what else to do. I still don't know what to do.'

Nisrin said, 'Whoever they are, they came here for a reason. There's only one place you'll find answers to this, the temple of Evren.'

GATHERED TOGETHER IN SUNETTE'S HOME, we retold our fears to Ntombi and Juna.

'We've got to get my daughter out of there,' Ntombi said, eyes on me. 'You could go with the keepers and take her back.'

'It's not as easy as that,' I said.

'Suni's right,' Juna said, pacing the room. 'Even if we could get Luna back, then what do we do? We don't need to see her to know she's getting worse. Lightning has sparked off three fires in the last two days. We have no idea how to help her.'

I reached for Ntombi's hand and gently squeezed. 'We don't know how to help Luna, but the temple might. I'll go with Zandi, see what we can find out. Until we get back, it's best Luna stays where she is. The townspeople would never accept her being released.'

Ntombi held my gaze and quietly said, 'Please find a way to help my daughter.'

26. Suni

ZANDI HAD NEVER BEEN OUT into open waters, and sat quietly at the stern as Nisrin and I paddled out to sea. Closing in on the outer rafts, people were busy reining in the day's catch, mending nets and gutting fish. I had always admired this peaceful way of life at sea, and looked out fondly over the tightknit community. In turn we were met with looks of apprehension, a reminder that the raft people were, on the whole, suspicious of outsiders. I had been here before, but that was a long time ago.

I recognised the man who came over to the dock as we sidled up alongside. Babacus had been a leader of the rafts when I had last boarded. I suspected it was still the case. He had a bullish presence, tall and well-built, with deep-set eyes peering out over a thick black beard now peppered with grey. If we were allowed passage, it would be on his word.

'What are you doing bringing these land dwellers aboard, Nisrin?' he said in a gravelly voice, looming over as we climbed up.

'We'll explain everything,' Nisrin said, straightening up to face him. 'But we must also speak with your father.'

'Not likely,' he said. 'My father's not well enough for company, you know that.' He paused as his gaze rested on me. 'I remember you. You're Mata's daughter.'

I nodded, keeping my eyes lowered.

'I wouldn't ask if it wasn't important,' Nisrin said. 'But the storm over Shendi is no natural storm. We need your father's counsel.'

'We should never have anchored here in the first place,' Babacus said, squinting out towards land. 'What curse has been raised here?'

'One that could affect land and sea,' Nisrin said.

Babacus adjusted his cap, pushing it back on his head as he looked at Nisrin. He hesitated then said, 'All right, see if my father will hear you out.'

He led the way across walkways and rope bridges deep into the rafts. Among colourful huts, the air was filled with the steady beats of giant pestles grinding grain into flour. Smoking fires roasted rows of fish on skewers. For the most part we received only sideways glances, apart from the broad smiles of children swimming in pools between the rafts.

Inside a hut, an old man was sleeping in a chair. Babacus went in, gently touching his father on the shoulder.

Nisrin followed, kneeling at the old man's feet as she said, 'I'm sorry to disturb you, Papa, but we need your counsel.' She looked over at me and Zandi standing in the doorway.

'Who's there?' the old man said, his words thick with sleep. As he squinted in my direction, I saw his cloudy eyes looking blindly into space.

'You remember Suni, Mata's daughter,' Nisrin said. 'She needs our help. Her land is in danger. She needs passage to the island of Evren.'

'Are you out of your mind!' Babacus said.

The old man wiped a hand across his eyes, cleared his throat and said, 'Hush lad and pass me some water. I want to hear what they've got to say.' He pushed himself up to sit straighter in the chair, accepted the mug Babacus handed him and took a long swig. He balanced the mug on his bony knee and turned to Nisrin. 'Tell me what business takes them to the islands?'

Nisrin spoke, uninterrupted, as she told of our plight.

Once she had finished, Babacus paced the length of the hut and said, 'The islands are a lawless place. No one looks to the temple anymore. It's not safe. You'll never make it past the docks.'

'Then you must go with them,' his father said.

Babacus paused, arms folded as he looked at his father. 'Why should we get involved?'

'Because they're speaking of the old religion, and no one should meddle with those powers. As raft people, we should remember that better than anyone.' The old man turned to face my direction. 'Our founders were once islanders. During the Great War, when dragons took to the skies, we were forced into exile at sea.'

I'd never heard the history of the rafts before.

'No one can be sure the founders came from the islands,' Babacus said. 'Those stories have been told a thousand different ways.'

'Details might change,' his father said, 'but the truth remains. And if the dragons wake, even the seas won't be safe.'

MASTS WERE HOISTED AND ANCHORS pulled: the floating town groaned to life. I was glad to feel the onset of an easterly breeze, since even in a high wind we faced a five-day sail.

I sat with Zandi at the edge of Nisrin's raft, sharpening arrowheads, watched by curious children on neighbouring rafts. Nisrin came to join us, bringing a platter of smoked fish.

'Keep going with the arrows,' she said, resting the tray in the middle of us as she sat down. 'Where we're going, we'll need them.'

'Is it really that bad?' Zandi asked.

'From what I've heard, people disappear at the docks,' Nisrin said. 'Murdered by gangs, so the rumours say.'

'What happened there?' I asked, helping myself to fish. 'Have the islands always been lawless?'

'Far from it.' Nisrin said. 'There was a time when the whole archipelago prospered from the coal on Drake Island. That's when the island of Evren gained its reputation as a main port of trade. You can still see gold-topped roofs on Evren's main street. But, when the mines ran dry, prosperity ended. Over the years, poverty set in.'

I threw the fish bones into the sea and licked the spicy marinade from my fingers. 'The Rayne Yangsens dress in fine clothes,' I said. 'They don't look like they come from a place of poverty and crime.'

Nisrin leaned back to rest on her hands. 'Well, it's been years since outsiders have been further than the docks. We don't know what it's like inland these days, except what we can see from the water.'

'Can you glimpse the temple from the sea?' Zandi asked.

'No,' Nisrin said. 'But we do know there's nothing grand about the temple, like there's nothing grand about the warders. Rumours have it, there are warders alive today who remember the age before the Great War, when the islands were covered in forest.'

'Hey!' A young girl called out from a neighbouring raft, smiling and waving. A woman, I presumed her mother, came out of the hut, scowling at me as she grabbed the girl's hand and ushered her back inside.

'Take no notice,' said Nisrin. 'The islands aren't a popular place. Most people think we shouldn't have taken you aboard.'

'Can't blame them,' Zandi said, as she picked up another arrowhead.

THAT NIGHT IN NISRIN'S HUT, curled in behind Zandi as she slept, I listened to the creaks and groans as we rose and fell with the tide. So far from home, I thought about Wanda alone in the valley as I slowly drifted to sleep.

RANDOM COLOURS OF THOUGHT CAME and went, before the colours slowly drained to grey and I arrived at the misty wall of *Serafay*. I stepped in, walking blind through the mist, until detecting the tunnel of moving air. I followed the channelling breeze and emerged from *Serafay* to find myself in the forest.

I recognised the place: the shape of the path and layout of surrounding bush and trees. But, for the first time since dreamwalking, Wanda wasn't there. My gaze was drawn to a single flower growing in the crevice of a mossy boulder. It took me a moment to realise why it stood out: its petals were bright indigo when I knew they should be pale blue. There were other things I realised were somehow wrong: all around, the colours of plant life were too light or too dark, or had a brown or grey tinge; and there was no birdsong, or any sound at all. Footsteps suddenly broke the quiet. I turned and saw Wanda running through the trees.

I ran after him down an overgrown path, deep into the forest. The further I went, a grey haze swept over the ground, like an early morning mist. It grew deeper, feeling cool against my legs, then my arms. At first, I thought it was *Serafay* come to claim me, but when it covered my face it felt like smoke stinging my eyes. The smoke grew so thick it was blinding. Disorientated, I listened for Wanda's footsteps, but aside from my own breathing, the forest was quiet. I held my arms out, slowly feeling my way through the trees, searching for clear air. Gradually, the smoke grew thin until it cleared, and I found myself standing in the middle of a forest glade.

EACH NIGHT ON THE RAFTS I searched for Wanda in the smoky forest, reliving the same dream that ended with me reaching the glade where the air was clear. Until the last night:

> I walked free of the smoke, arriving in the forest glade, when I heard Wanda's voice cry out, 'Luna!'
>
> I looked around at the surrounding trees, searching for him, but I couldn't see through the wall of smoke edging the glade. I opened my mouth to call his name, but I had no voice in the dream world. Cracking and spitting, like burning wood, sounded distant at first, but was coming closer. A flicker of orange appeared in the smoke, before a burst of fire came sweeping through the trees. Hearing running footsteps, I looked around, but in the confusion, I couldn't tell which direction they were coming from. Desperate to guide Wanda to safety, I closed my eyes and looked into the abyss. Sparks of light appeared to me like stars in a night sky. I focused on one shining brighter than the rest, watched it glow brighter as I willed it towards me. When its light was all I could see, I opened my eyes. Wanda was standing next to me, while all around the forest burned.

27. Wanda

SINCE RELEASING THE TUFTED TAMARIN, I had returned to the forest several times, checking on its progress. It was doing well, but despite my efforts to call it to me, it kept its distance. It was the same with every creature I tried to reach out to: from adders in the grass to pine warblers in the trees. Was it because they sensed the shadow? After the Mantra had turned its back on me, the cool touch of the shadow was permanently wrapped around my skin, closer than it had ever been.

Alone with the shadow, with each day that passed, I felt myself becoming increasingly detached from the land that had always kept me grounded. A cold well of emptiness swelled inside, leaving my stomach permanently growling in hunger. No amount of fruit, roots and berries could relieve my aching belly. I had tried fighting against my cravings for fresh meat, afraid of where it would lead, but driven by pangs of hunger I finally lost my will.

Trekking across the plains, a breeze brushed through tall grasses, filling the air with a gentle 'hush'. Swayed by the natural sound, sudden tears pricked my eyes but I blinked them away. Finally, I spotted an unsuspecting hare. I crouched down in the grass and armed my catapult. I crept in closer, let loose the stone and watched the hare go down. I retrieved my kill and took it back to the cave.

The droning hum of screeching, humming and clicking echoed out of the shadow's dark depths as it clung to my skin. My hands moved in time with the rise and fall of its rhythm, as I slowly peeled away the skin. With each strip of skin I pulled back, my gaze lingered on the pattern of blood vessels marking the flesh. Finally, I raised the hare to my lips, stared straight ahead and bit down on raw flesh. I sucked the bones clean and tossed them aside, then sank back into the shadow's cool embrace as its song transformed into a sweet melody.

As the notes rose and fell, my stomach turned with nausea, mild at first, but then my vision blurred and my head felt like I was spinning. I closed my eyes, feeling a strange tingling in my skin as the feel of the cold stone cave drifted, until I felt like I was floating in mid-air. I searched with my hands to feel the physical world, but found nothing solid to hold onto. Feeling the nausea lift, I opened my eyes and looked out into dark that stretched all around, vast like the sky. A flash of orange ripped a hole in the dark, forming a band of light surrounding a gaping black hole. As though swept into a current, I began moving towards it, drifting through until I was encircled by light. I shut my eyes, convinced I must be dreaming. When I opened them again, I felt myself suddenly drop.

Darkness turned to blue sky as I entered another world, the rush of wind roaring in my ears as I fell through the sky towards open sea. Until a sudden jolt, then a lift, scooped me up out of my fall. I felt the cool leathery skin of what carried me, scaled, like a reptile. Rushing air sounded like giant wings beating. But to my eyes it was a confusing sight: with an appearance almost perfectly camouflaged, the creature was impossible to identify. Its colours were constantly changing: masked by a silvery sheen, at times the body appeared to reflect the surroundings. As we plunged down into a wide arc, skimming the surface of the sea, I looked out across the creature's changing silhouette and saw only that it was vast.

Fast approaching the cliff-face of an island, I clung to what felt like bony spines as we climbed. Rounding the cliffs, I looked out across the sloping landscape where great plumes of smoke hung low over a forest in flames. Flying over forest clearings levelled by fire, seeing corpses strewn among blackened trees and burnt-out ruins, screams filled the air. We flew on, over an inlet of sea to the shores of another island, and another. There were five islands in all, and they were all burning.

Sickened, I closed my eyes, at a loss to know why I should see such horrors. Behind closed eyes, a woman appeared to me. With pale white skin, flaming red hair and piercing blue eyes, she was like no one I had seen before. Gazing at her face, a thought, a word, entered my head. I looked into her eyes and called her by her name, Evren. As the word left my lips, I felt cold stone beneath me. I opened my eyes to find myself back in the cave.

VISIONS OF THE WOMAN RETURNED over the coming days, along with thoughts and sensations that were out of place: the smell of sea air and wet grass; the sound of water lapping over pebbles; a soft thud, like a heavy wooden door closing, followed by climbing footsteps echoing against stone steps. It was like glimpsing a person's memories. I didn't know how or why, it just was.

I knew what it was to enter a creature's mind and see the world through their eyes. I wondered if the same was happening to me, wondered if a seed had been planted in my mind. And I thought about Luna. Was Evren the same woman Luna had seen in the shadow? My cousin talked about dragons. Was it possible that's what had carried me in my vision? More than ever I felt the significance of the bond with my cousin. It was a thought that plagued my dream one night:

It was the morning after a night camping with Luna in our favourite spot in the forest. Luna's imprint in the bed of aloe grass was still warm, but she was nowhere to be seen. I called her name but there was no reply. The forest was strangely silent. I looked up into the trees but could see no birds. I looked around at the surrounding foliage, confused by subtle changes: the leaves of a sprawling olive bush were tinged brown; the caps of white speckled, panther cap mushrooms were dull grey; and moss covering rocks was sickly yellow when it should be deep green.

I got up and headed down the path in search of Luna, slowing when I saw what looked like smoke drifting out of the undergrowth.

'Wanda!'

I turned in the direction of Luna's frightened voice. She called again and again. Guided by her voice, I veered onto a different path. Smoke came spilling out from the undergrowth, swirling around my feet then my knees, becoming so deep it covered up to my waist. I stopped, alarmed and confused. There were no other signs of a fire.

'Luna, where are you?' I called.

'I'm over here!'

Now she sounded her usual relaxed self; it seemed odd considering the forest was filling with smoke.

'Stay where you are,' I said. 'I'll come to you.'

I pulled my scarf up over my mouth and nose, breathing into my hand, as Luna guided me deeper into the smoke. Eyes stinging, I squinted into the thick haze, stumbling blindly through the trees. Approaching the clearing, the smoke grew thin. I rubbed my watering eyes and stepped out of the trees to where the air was clear. Luna was waiting for me in the forest clearing, smiling as though nothing was amiss. When she held her hand out to me, I hesitated and glanced back into the trees. The smoke was gone.

'Come on,' she said. 'I've got something to show you.'

She led the way into the trees on the far side, where sunlight filtered down through the canopy, and birdsong rang in the air all around. A song warbler was singing to her eggs in the low branch of an acatcha tree. I followed Luna as she climbed up to the nest. The song warbler flew up, watching from a high branch as we peered at her eggs.

'They're about to hatch,' I said, seeing cracks appear in the blue speckled shell.

The light grew suddenly dim when cloud cover moved in.

'It's here,' Luna said in a low voice.

I looked at her, confused by the apparent change: kneeling back on her heels, staring straight up, she appeared frozen in fear. Then, without warning, she swung down from the branch and ran off into the forest.

I climbed down and ran after, calling for her to stop, but she didn't answer. I soon lost all sign of her and slowed to a walk, calling out her name. Aside from the sound of my own footsteps, the forest was silent again. Smoke came drifting out from the undergrowth, growing deeper the further I went. When it covered up to my knees, Luna finally answered.

'Wanda, I'm here.'

Now she sounded playful, as though it was a game of hide and seek. Rounding a corner, I saw her up ahead on the path.

'I'm here,' she said again.

I stopped, frightened by the sound of two voices speaking at once from her lips: one sounded like Luna, the other like an old man. The scar on her cheek was glowing, red and inflamed, swelling until the fine lines patterning the scar started to crack with orange light shining through. She started giggling like a child when she slowly lifted off the ground, hovering mid-air with her arms spread out at her sides. When her hair started to smoulder, laughter turned to confusion. And when the scar on her cheek burst open, revealing a ball of fire under her skin, fear shone from her eyes. A flame sparked in her hair, and another, lighting a fire that fanned her head. She stared at me in horror when her body jerked with a sudden movement that tilted her back. A moment later she shot backwards, dragged into the trees as though by an unseen force. 'Luna!' I yelled, staring after her smouldering trail, but she was gone.

I set off running after her, not knowing whether I should be afraid of my cousin, or the forest. Smoke came thick and fast, blinding my way, forcing me to stop. I called her name again and again, straining to hear a sign. But aside from my own heavy breathing, I heard nothing. I bent forwards, hands on my knees, squinting into the grey haze, wondering whether I would ever see my cousin again. Helpless against powers I didn't understand, I was lost in a place that should be as familiar as home.

A faint flicker of white light appeared in the smoky air. Seeing something so out of place, I focused on it, imagining it was a sign. I held my arms out, feeling my way through the trees, following the light that grew brighter the closer I came. It guided me to the edge of a glade where the air was clear. Stepping out of the trees, I stopped and stared in surprise. Suni was there, appearing like a ghost, holding the orb of light in her cupped hands. I walked towards her but she was looking beyond me, into the trees. I turned and saw the forest on fire.

I WOKE, DRENCHED IN A cold sweat. My stomach turned with sickly dread as I stared up at the roof of the cave, replaying the dream over and over in my head. Slowly I sat up and turned to look at the world outside. Luna was lost and, somehow, I had to find her.

28. Suni

HUDDLED WITH ZANDI IN NISRIN'S hut, wrapped in warm shawls provided by others, we could still feel wisps of a cold westerly wind seep through cracks in the slats. As I told about Wanda and the forest on fire, I took comfort in Zandi's reassurances: the dream was surely nothing more than my own fears reimagined. We were heading into the unknown, our minds filled with stories of fire breathing dragons, tales so vivid and extraordinary they had sparked a recurring dream.

The further west we travelled, the rougher the sea became. Choppy waters turned a murky green/brown, and Zandi and I both struggled with nausea as the rafts rose and fell on ocean swells, overlooked by a dull grey sky. Finally, on the morning of the fifth day, sails were lowered and anchors dropped, while the rafts creaked and groaned to a stop. Standing at the edge of the rafts with Zandi and Nisrin, we looked out at the island of Evren.

It was edged by a long quay, with grey stone docks and river ships and boats of every kind: long boats that Nisrin explained were used to transport goods between the islands, and larger sailing vessels for trade further afield. Beyond the docks, the steep hillside was crammed with stone buildings: clusters of gold dome roofs and emerald green spires gave splashes of colour to the rest that were grey.

'Evren's the largest of the islands,' Nisrin said. 'The others stretch out behind it. The temple is just over the hill.'

Zandi looked out with a hand cupped over her brow. 'Can't we get to the temple from the other side of the island, if the docks are as bad as you say they are?'

'The docks are the only way in,' Nisrin said. 'The other side of the island is cliffs with no way up.'

Babacus arrived with his sons, Curtis and Trent, all wearing belts laden with knives. 'We can expect no welcome here,' he said. 'As far as I know, gangs run these shores.' He glanced at the fishing knife tied to Nisrin's waist, and the bows and arrows Zandi and I carried. 'I hope you women know how to use those.'

'We'll manage,' Zandi said with a curt smile.

'Well, just keep your wits about you,' Babacus said. 'If we take anyone else, we'll attract too much attention. As it is, we'll have to watch each other's backs.'

We paddled to the dock in two canoes, pulling in between longboats laden with shellfish. Once the canoes were secured, we set off through the crowds of traders and sailors. They appeared no more threatening than the sailors we were used to seeing back home, but as Babacus led the way down a cobbled street edged with tall grey buildings, he had his hand rested on the hilt of his knife.

The street branched into narrow alleyways, deserted except for rats scurrying among waste packaging and fish bones. The deeper we went, the buildings appeared abandoned, littered with broken windows. Up ahead someone was slumped against a wall. I thought he was sleeping, but as we approached, not even the fishy smell of the docks could mask the stench of the dead body. Dressed in rags his emaciated body was covered in sores, his skin was grey, and his open eyes lifeless.

'Keep moving,' Babacus said, leading us on. 'There's nothing anyone can do for him now.'

Turning the corner, seeing more bodies lying on the ground like discarded litter, I felt the urge to wretch. But when I saw a young boy, clinging to the arm of a dead woman I presumed was his mother, I swallowed the sickly feeling and went towards him. He saw me coming, jumped up and ran away.

'This man's alive,' Zandi said. The body at her feet looked like a corpse, until his staring eyes blinked, his lips parted, and he tried to raise an arm.

'What happened here,' I said. 'These aren't violent gangs. These people need help.'

'They're beyond help,' Trent said. 'It looks like some sort of plague.' He turned away from the sight of rats gnawing a dead man's face, bent forward and was sick. 'We shouldn't be here,' he said, wiping his mouth.

'Look out,' Babacus said.

Three men were walking towards us. With malnourished bodies, gaunt faces, and an unfriendly glint in their eyes, they reminded me of the outcasts back home. They each pulled out a knife as they came near.

'Back off,' Zandi said, nocking an arrow.

We all followed her lead, grouping together, brandishing our weapons. The assailants stopped as though considering their chances.

'Spare a few coins and we'll be on our way,' one man said, holding out a hand, while keeping the knife raised in the other.

I threw a handful of coins onto the ground at his feet. 'That's all there is. Take it and leave.'

All three dropped down, grabbing at the coins.

'Keep moving,' Babacus said in a low voice, ushering us on.

We veered right, down an alley that opened out into the deserted main street. Climbing the hill, leaving the oppressive atmosphere of the docks behind us, we passed some strange and intriguing sights. Around the main street, and down branching cobbled lanes, dried-out fountains and buildings covered in faded murals portrayed winged dragons with fiery breath and lean bodies in writhing poses. Babacus said the artwork was centuries old. It was the first time I had seen dragons depicted; here they were embedded into the fabric of the town.

At the brow of the hill, we came to a wealthy neighbourhood that was in stark contrast to the impoverished docks. Big houses stood in courtyards secured behind high metal gates, where large and frowning men stood guard. Beyond the houses, we reached the edge of town, where rough ground skirted heathland that stretched to the edge of this high peninsula. Out across the heath stood the grey stone, fortress walls of the temple.

The sound of crashing waves carried on the fresh sea breeze, as we cut down a narrow path through fern and gorse bushes tipped with purple flowers. Gathered at the wooden gate, Babacus rang the bell hanging from the gatepost. In answer to the loud clang, a hatch in the gate opened and an old man looked out. With a bald head and straggly white beard to match his pale complexion, there was suspicion in his squinting eyes. I suspected the temple didn't receive many visitors.

'What do you want?' he asked.

'We've come to ask for counsel from the temple,' I said.

He fixed his eyes on me. 'You don't come from here.'

'No, but…'

'Then you've no business being here.'

He went to slam the hatch closed, but Zandi pushed it back and said, 'We've come a long way.'

'Reynauld,' said a woman's voice from inside. 'Who's at the gate?'

The old man turned, the back of his head blocking our view through the hatch.

'Strangers seeking counsel with the temple, Madam,' he said. 'They're not from here. I've told them they're not welcome.'

There was a pause before the man disappeared and, in his place, a woman looked out. She had a striking appearance, with piercing blue eyes, pale white skin, and white hair peppered with grey. On first glance I thought she looked no older than me, a woman approaching thirty, but there was maturity in her colouring and wisdom in her eyes that made it difficult to place her.

'Where do you come from?' she asked, her eyes shining with intrigue.

'A land called Shendi, far from here,' I said. 'We need the help of the temple.'

She quietly considered each of us in turn, before snapping the hatch shut. A moment later, the gate opened.

29. Suni

FOR ALL ITS MYSTERY, THE temple had a surprisingly simple design. Standing in the centre of a stone courtyard, it was a single-storey building without even windows to add interest to the sprawling plain grey walls. As Reynauld closed the gate behind us, I considered the woman who welcomed us. She had a curious appearance. Tall and slim, her long straight hair was styled in a way I had not seen before: shaved high up the sides and left long at the top, tied into a plait reaching down the length of her back. Barefoot, she wore a simple grey smock with a woollen shawl draped over her shoulders, and a silver chain around her neck with a locket encrusted with emeralds.

'Please forgive Reynauld's suspicion,' the woman said. 'Few people grace our gates, and we're not used to strangers.' Her gaze rested on me. 'You say your land is far from here?'

'Yes,' I said. 'We sailed five days from the east. My name is Suni and this is Zandi. Our friends are of the raft people; they gave us passage.'

There was kindness in her smile and curiosity in her eyes as she said, 'Your introductions are brief. I've heard of lands of the far east. Your people put little value on names.'

I had grown up hearing of places where names were given not only to people, but also to rivers, forests, mountains and plains. My mother had taught me that naming implied ownership; the land gave us a home, food and shelter, it was not ours to own.

'And what's your name?' Zandi asked.

I stiffened hearing her sharp tone, but the woman seemed unfazed.

'I am Eleanor Yin Slyte, a priestess of the temple.' She turned to Nisrin, Babacus and his sons. 'The raft people were once our people. You are all welcome, but your weapons must remain at the gate. No harm will come to you within these walls.'

'I'll keep my weapons and wait here,' Babacus said.

'As you like,' the priestess said, with a slight nod.

Babacus stayed behind with his sons, while the rest of us followed the priestess across the courtyard.

Rounding the eastern wall, we arrived at an arched doorway where two stone dragons stood either side. Eleanor pushed the wooden doors open and led us into the huge entrance hall, where we were met with an unexpected sight. Lit by candlelight, mosaic tiles covered the curved walls from floor to ceiling, creating colourful designs on an impressive scale. As I looked around at the intricate work, our footsteps echoed in the cool air that felt filled with a magical aura.

A girl was standing on top of a ladder propped against one wall. Like Eleanor, she wore a simple grey smock and had the same pale white skin, but her hair matched the orange colouring of Adela Rayne Yangsen's. She didn't look up from her work, cementing a new layer of tiles over the old, carefully smoothing down mortar between the cracks.

'That is Sylvie, one of our apprentices,' Eleanor said. 'We all take our turn to maintain the temple walls.'

Intrigued by the secrets of the temple, I reached out, brushing my fingers over a floral pattern of blue.

'Don't disturb the tiles,' Eleanor said, gently pushing my hand away. She added a reassuring smile. 'Many hands have laboured over these walls.'

'I've just never seen anything like it before,' I said, looking around the hall. 'It's all so colourful, like the artwork in the streets.'

'The colours maybe bright,' Eleanor said, 'but they hide a dark and powerful history that is largely forgotten in the modern world. The murals on the streets were painted long ago, when people still remembered the cause of their suffering.'

'The dragons,' Nisrin said.

Eleanor nodded. 'There was a time when the gifts were common among our people: those with the power to see without time, or speak with animals, or commune with the winds.' She led us to a scene depicted in the mosaic. As she continued with her account, we saw the stories of history revealed in the tiles. 'We prided ourselves on being the origin of gifts born from the time of the mages. But it was the gifted among us who were most vulnerable to the dragons.' She paused, looking at me with an intense gaze that lingered. 'As warders we work tirelessly to keep the dragons from waking, but even while they sleep, they have the power to break a gifted mind. In the time when gifts were commonplace, people suffered visions that slowly drove them mad.' She pulled the shawl tighter around her shoulders and fingered the locket at her throat. 'They lived in fear and were too afraid to sleep or dream. Some became so desperate, they jumped to their death at the cliffs. The murals and sculptures you saw on the streets were created out of desperation, to pay homage to the dragons. People believed that replicating their image would show honour and subservience, and would appease the dragons.' She paused then added, 'But that was a long time ago.'

'And now?' I asked.

'Now the temple is forgotten by the modern world, but we continue with our work regardless. As for the islands, you've seen for yourselves what these lands have become.'

'People at the docks seem to be suffering some sort of plague,' Nisrin said.

'It's no plague,' Eleanor said. 'What you've seen are people ravaged by Papaver, or at least a version of it.' She paused, considering our blank faces. 'It originates from a flower that grows here. Its medicinal properties have been used for centuries to relieve pain and calm an anxious mind, giving respite from visions brought on by the dragons. But in recent years the flower was farmed and manipulated, and the seeds crushed down and brewed into a potion that destroys the mind. Now we have a population of desperate addicts, and streets run by gangs making a fortune from the trade.' Her eyes rested on me, with a stare so intense I felt unnerved. 'Knowing the temple is responsible for the islands' ruin, is our shame. It was one of our own, a boy we took in and sheltered.' She lay a hand on my shoulder. 'I think you know the man who turned on us: Brahim Rayne Yangsen.'

My mouth turned dry.

'Brahim, Adela and Ray arrived at my homeland,' I quietly said, wondering about the depth of her gift.

She slowly nodded. 'Their parents were gifted and driven to madness by the dragons. They took their own lives at the cliffs, leaving behind three orphaned children.'

'Were the children gifted?' Zandi asked.

Eleanor shook her head. 'Brahim was fifteen when he came to us, asking to serve the old religion. Skies be merciful, we pitied him and took him on as an apprentice. He was intelligent but unruly, and wasn't here long. He ended up trading in Papaver down at the docks with Adela and Ray.' I reached for Zandi's hand as Eleanor continued. 'Brahim was never content with anything. He started experimenting with the flower, strengthening its effect, turning it into the potent form you see on the streets. We failed him. And now the Rayne Yangsens make their fortune from other people's suffering.'

'There has been sickness among men on my homeland,' I said. 'It's an illness we couldn't explain, but it effects the body and mind. It's not unlike what we saw at the docks, although not as bad.'

Eleanor nodded, frowning as she said, 'They've been dealing with sea traders for years. I'm sorry to know it affects your homeland.'

'But the men back home seem to be recovering,' I said. 'The Rayne Yangsens have been giving out some sort of cure.'

'They have no cures,' Eleanor said. 'Only more Papaver.' She put a hand on my arm and gently squeezed. Her lips didn't move but I heard her voice speaking inside my head: '*Dreamwalker.*' I stared into her eyes, unnerved by her powers. 'The Rayne Yangsens aren't the only reason you're here.' She turned to Zandi and Nisrin. 'Come with me, all of you. I think you should meet my father.'

30. Suni

ELEANOR LED THE WAY DOWN one of several branching hallways, where more mosaic covered every inch of stone. I followed behind Zandi and Nisrin, considering our mysterious host and her powers as a warder; what strange connection existed between us that enabled her to speak inside my head? She had the appearance of youth but the wisdom of age. I felt that wisdom in the temple walls, in the history of the layered tiles.

I stopped, distracted by faint whispering that seemed to be coming from the wall. Seeing a grey haze drifting out between the tiles, I reached out to touch it with my fingers. It looked and felt like cool mist.

'What is this?' I asked.

Zandi and Nisrin were looking at me puzzled.

'Don't you see it? Don't you hear it?'

They shook their heads.

I turned to Eleanor who was quietly watching from further down the corridor. Her mouth was closed, her lips didn't move, but I heard her voice speaking inside my head: '*You who sees the mists of Serafay.*' As she turned to continue on down the corridor, she said out loud, 'The fabric of the temple is older than you can imagine.'

Zandi slipped her hand in mine and led me on to catch up with the priestess.

'The temple has thirteen priests and priestesses warding,' Eleanor said, 'and three transcending.'

'What do you mean, transcending?' Zandi asked, as we gathered together outside a door with dragons carved into the wood.

'You will see,' Eleanor said. 'This is my father's room. He is one of our transcenders. Be quiet when we enter: I must wake him slowly.'

She opened the door into a musty room, where dust lay thick over shelves stuffed with books and vials. Mosaic tiles covered from floor to ceiling, except for the far wall that was not like anything I had seen before. It had a leathery appearance, mottled with shades of green and brown, and was moving: rising and falling in a steady rhythm, as though it was breathing. We stayed by the desk in the corner of the room, while Eleanor went over and placed a gentle hand on the moving wall.

'Father,' she softly said.

I watched in amazement as two eyes opened, looking out from the wall. At first, they appeared like fiery red orbs, but as they focused on Eleanor, they faded to yellow with black slit pupils. The wall bulged and the shape of a head, shoulders and torso pushed out. The facial features appeared to be human, but with two bony protrusions on its forehead like horns, and skin the same mottled leather as the wall. I wondered what it was.

The creature opened its mouth, revealing yellowed fangs. A human voice asked, 'My daughter, have I slept long?'

'You're peaceful, father,' Eleanor said.

The creature slowly blinked then turned his gaze onto me.

'She has a gift,' Eleanor said. 'And they need our help.' She held her hand out, beckoning me to her. 'Come closer. Don't be afraid.'

I stepped slowly towards her, keeping my eyes on the creature. He had a chain around his neck, holding a locket like the one Eleanor wore. Eleanor put her hands on my shoulders, guiding me to stand in front of her father.

'You are wise to fear the beast,' the creature said. 'But I was once just a man.' He brought his face closer to mine, closed his eyes and inhaled, as though smelling me. 'Dreamwalker,' he said, as he breathed out. When he opened his eyes, the slit black pupils widened into ovals. 'You have seen a dragon transcending.' He held me fixed in his gaze, until his eyes suddenly flicked to the side, darkening to red. Fear washed over his face, as he sank back, cowering. 'The shadows are here.'

Eleanor came forward and lay a hand on her father's brow. 'You need to sleep now,' she softly said. She reached for the locket hanging at his throat and gently pressed it against his chest. 'Sleep, father.'

As though soothed by her voice and her touch, his eyes returned to yellow before he closed them. Watching him sink back into the wall, I tried to comprehend a life so intrinsically part of the temple. I glanced at Eleanor, at a loss to know what it would be like to have a father that was only part human. Seeing a distant longing in her eyes, I wondered what memories she clung to from when he had been a man.

Eleanor put a hand on my shoulder, and guided us all back out into the hallway.

'What happened to your father?' I asked, as she closed the door behind us.

'My father was once a man, gifted as a mage. Like the mages that came before him, his gift led him to the dragon. Now he is a hybrid, part man/part dragon, and I am his warder.' She brushed a hand against the door. 'I keep my father from completing the transformation. There was a time when he would walk freely, but as years passed, he grew too afraid to leave his room. All our hybrids have retreated to the walls.'

'How is this possible?' Zandi said.

Eleanor softly smiled and said, 'You came in search of our temple, but it is strange to you. Here we work with dreams. Keeping my father content in his dream controls the dragon, and keeps the man alive. But my father will never again breathe fresh air.' She paused, gazing into space before looking at me. 'Life in the temple is all I have ever known. But now I meet you, Suni from the far east. My father sees in you more than you know, and you have seen more than you realise.'

31. Suni

ELEANOR PLACED A HAND ON my arm and said, 'Tell me what you know about Brahim?'

'He claims to be a warder of this temple,' I said. 'He spoke about the Dragon Lands and said that during the Great War, one of the dragons fled the islands and has been sleeping in the mountains of my homeland ever since.'

'May the good gifts keep us safe,' she whispered as though to herself. She paused, gazing into my eyes, then stepped back, sweeping her arm out to the side as she glanced around the walls. 'The site of this temple is where it all began. It was built from the ruins of the castle that was once Evren's home. During the Great War, when Evren turned from mage to dragon form, the castle was destroyed and Evren left these lands.' She looked back to face us. 'The cellars are all that remain of the original building. We maintain the walls and floors with tiles to ward against powerful magic that lies buried down there. Evren unlocked the oldest of weaves when she called forth the mists of *Serafay*.'

'The elders of our homeland weave the mist,' Zandi said.

'A spell, nothing more,' Eleanor said. 'Only the dead or a dreamwalker can know *Serafay*, the corridor between dreams.' Her eyes rested on me. 'The mists of *Serafay* cannot be manipulated into weaves. Nor can they be banished once they've been brought into being. We built this temple out of rock and stone, but beneath our labour, the foundations are organic. There's much we don't understand. But we work tirelessly to keep the mist out, since the transcenders fear shadows they see in it.'

She glanced briefly at the door of her father's room, before turning back to face me. 'Dreamwalking is a gift that leads you to know the mists. But the mists are more powerful than even you can imagine. Somehow, they were the origin of the dragon's power, the origin of all transformations.' She put a hand on my arm. 'You've seen it before, on your homeland: you've seen a transcender.'

I shook my head, confused.

She gazed at me with a penetrating stare. 'We ward for all the dragons, but until now, we didn't know where Evren lay. The Rayne Yangsens are not warders, but something led them to your land. You have a hybrid among your people.'

'We've never seen a hybrid before today,' Zandi said. 'The Rayne Yangsens arrived after hearing about Luna, a girl that has nightmares and talks about the coming of a dragon.'

'She's powerful,' I said. 'It's hard to explain, but it's like she brought the storm. Brahim told us that she's dangerous because she's an untrained warder. They said they can train her to channel her powers to ward for the dragon in the mountains.' I paused, then added, 'We handed her over to them.'

Eleanor quietly considered us for a moment, then said, 'What you describe, it sounds more likely that Luna is gifted with the powers of a mage and has started down the path of transcendence.' No one answered. The thought of Luna destined for the same fate as Eleanor's father was unthinkable. 'Come with me,' Eleanor said. 'I want to show you something.'

She led us back through the temple, out into the courtyard, and through a narrow gate on the far side. The path led out across the clifftops, to a beacon built close to the edge. We climbed the spiralling steps and gathered around the fire at the top, glad of the warmth against the cold wind.

'Out there,' Eleanor said, pointing west across the seascape.

'The Dragon Lands,' Nisrin said.

It was a cloudless, dull grey sky, but over a barren island, low lying storm clouds swirled around a dark centre.

'It's the place where four dragons lay sleeping,' Eleanor said. 'Even in sleep, they have the power to keep the storm alive.'

'It looks like the storm over Shendi,' Zandi said.

Watching streaks of white lightning flash over the Dragon Lands, with the cold westerly wind whistling in my ears, I began to hear a harmony of notes in the wind, slowly forming a haunting melody: '*Oraaag*.'

'Do you hear that?' I said.

'It's the curse,' Nisrin said. 'These waters are deadly.'

'The dragon song lures sailors to their death,' Eleanor said, 'since death feeds the power of the dragons. We do what we can, keeping the beacon lit as a warning to stay away from these waters.'

'But I can hear a word in the wind,' I said. 'It's saying 'Orag'.'

'I hear it too,' Zandi said, eyes narrowed as she looked at me.

I turned to Eleanor. 'You call the dragon on my homeland, Evren, but for years we knew it as Orag. It was the name spoken by a mad King who once ruled our land.'

'And was this King gifted?' Eleanor asked.

'Yes,' I said. 'He was gifted to speak the tongue of animals.'

Eleanor paused, looking out to sea. 'Some years ago, warders for Evren sensed a trespasser in the dream. Then one day the trespasser was gone. Until recently.' Her eyes narrowed as she looked back at me. 'Evren must have sensed the King's gift and reached out to him, giving him the word of Orag. It's a spell, the most forbidden of spells, performed to bring about a dragon's awakening. But to an untrained mind, speaking with a dragon can lead to madness.'

I thought of the King we had found in the palace dungeons, ravaged by the dark spirit, reduced to babbling nonsense. And the eerie sound that accompanied him: chirping, screeching and droning, like the clicks and wingbeats of a massive insect swarm. The same noise had surrounded Luna, the night we saw her possessed.

'Is it possible that the dragon is speaking to Luna?' I asked.

'I can't be sure,' Eleanor said. 'But either way, you say the storm over the Dragon Lands resembles the storm over your homeland, a storm brought by Luna. Only a mage on the path of transcendence can bring about such a storm. Luna may not realise what is happening to her, but the Rayne Yangsens do. It's why they went looking for her.'

'But you said the Rayne Yangsens are ungifted,' Zandi said.

Eleanor pulled the shawl tight around her, wrapping her arms around her waist as she looked out towards the temple. 'Brahim was asked to leave the temple when we found him in the chamber of scrolls; a forbidden place for an apprentice. He was looking through our most ancient scriptures, where the spell of Orag is written.' She paused, then said, 'The scriptures tell that if one who is gifted performs the spell, they will bring about an awakening. And if ungifted, a circle of three can lead to the same end.' She slowly turned to face us. 'I think Brahim wants to take Luna's transcendence to completion. He wants her to become the dragon.'

I stared into her eyes, struggling to comprehend what she was saying. But her gaze did not falter.

'But why?' I said. 'If Luna is what you say she is, why would they want to see her transform?'

Eleanor said, 'I've never heard of a child with these powers before, and my knowledge of the scriptures is limited. We must speak with my elders.'

32. Suni

ELEANOR TOOK US TO THE chamber of scrolls, a large, cavernous library filled floor to ceiling with shelving, stuffed with dusty rolls of parchment. Beyond this, the chamber opened out further into a seating area, with chairs arranged in a circle. Waiting for the priests and priestesses to arrive, I studied the mosaic mural on the wall behind us. It pictured a dragon perched on a towering crag, looking out across the forest slope, eyes narrowed into slits, focused, as though spying prey among the trees. Wisps of smoke drifted from flaring nostrils, its jaws slightly parted exposing yellowed fangs, its angular head deep red, the colour of blood blended into green down its long neck. Balanced by a lowered tail tipped with spines, its leathery wings were poised for flight. My gaze drifted to the silhouettes of three other dragons flying in the distant skies.

Thirteen priests and priestesses arrived and took their seats. Two, a man and woman, appeared youthful like Eleanor, but the rest looked much older. Among the hunched shoulders, sagging skin and wisps of hair on balding scalps, I imaged a number of them had seen well over a century come and go. Their watery grey eyes fixed on Eleanor as she spoke about all that had transpired since our arrival.

When she finished speaking, an old man named Crandor turned to me and said, 'Dreamwalking is an ancient gift, rooted in a powerful bloodline. It is something we haven't known since the age of dragons. Is it your only gift?'

'Yes,' I said, nervously clearing my throat.

He leaned forward in his chair. 'Can you speak with the creatures? Have you seen the eye of fire? Does the sky around you turn to storm?'

I shook my head, confused.

Eleanor said to him, 'My father saw the gift of a dreamwalker, nothing more.'

Crandor glanced at the old woman sitting next to him, then looked back at me and said, 'Beatrice and I are warders for Evren. We have sensed a trespasser in the dragon's dream, knowingly or unknowingly working against us. Dreamwalking is a powerful gift. We need to be sure it's not you: an untrained warder straying into a dragon's dream will find only madness.'

I looked at him blankly, feeling my cheeks grow warm.

'She has no knowledge of the dragon's dream,' Eleanor said. She looked at me with a gentle smile. 'Yours is a powerful gift, with intimate knowledge of the mists of *Serafay*, the source of the dragons' creation.'

With Crandor's suspicious gaze still fixed on me, I looked away, finding distraction in the mural.

'You say there are five dragons,' I said. 'But in the picture there are only four.'

'It is Evren who is missing,' Eleanor said. 'The only female dragon.'

'She is absent from all our records,' Beatrice added. 'As the temple's scribe, I have read every scroll in this chamber, dating back to the time before the dragons. There is history recorded of all the mages, both as men before their transformations, and as dragons. But not Evren. We have no knowledge of what she looked like, as a woman or a dragon.' She paused then said, 'Here on the islands, history wasn't kind to women. It is likely *Serafay* wasn't the only source of the dragon's creation.'

'That is opinion rather than fact,' an old man said.

Beatrice kept her eyes on me. 'I'm referring to stories passed down from mothers to daughters through the ages, that tell of a woman's life during Evren's time, and how Evren was the first to discover the power of the dragons. Before my time, scribes were men and those stories were either never written or the records disappeared.' The same old man grumbled out loud, but Beatrice continued regardless. 'Without knowing the facts of Evren's true history, we cannot know the origin of the dragons. That is why, as warders, we do nothing more than bandage a festering wound.'

'That's as may be,' Crandor said. 'But our gift still keeps the world safe from dragons.'

Sensing disquiet in the room, I asked, 'Your gift as warders, how do you keep the dragons sleeping?'

Eleanor said, 'We share the dream of the dragon or hybrid we ward for, and lay wards in the dream.' She held out the locket on the chain around her neck. Two other warders wore a similar jewel. 'Those of us warding for hybrids wear lockets containing a lock of our own hair and a lock of our loved one. Warded, it holds our connection strong, acting as an amulet to guide us to the dream.' She stood up, leaving the circle as she went to an old chest in the corner. 'Those who ward for dragons keep their amulets in here.'

She lifted the lid and beckoned us over. Inside, we saw a curious collection of old bones that looked like huge teeth and claws.

'They were collected from the Dragon Lands,' Eleanor said. 'Teeth, claws and scales shed by the dragons act as amulets.' She carefully sifted through the bones. 'Warding for Evren was always the most difficult. For many years, we had no amulet to help strengthen the connection.' She lifted her hand out and held up a stone I recognised. 'This crystal was traded at the docks and found its way to us. We soon discovered its powers as an amulet for Evren.'

'I know this stone,' I said, leaning in for a closer look. 'I once used it to buy passage on the rafts.' I thought back to those nights, years ago, when gazing into the crystal showed me the path to *Serafay*, where my mother would be waiting. It had once been a familiar treasure. Now, hearing it was a dragon's amulet, I was wary of its power. 'I found it in the crystal mines in the mountains back home.'

'The mountains where Evren lies sleeping,' Eleanor said, slowly nodding as she looked at the crystal.

'Yes,' I quietly said, stunned to think how our two worlds were connected.

Zandi put her hand on my shoulder and said, 'I still don't see what any of this has got to do with Luna. Or what the Rayne Yangsens want from her.'

'They want power,' Crandor said, pausing as we resumed our seats. 'If Luna transforms into the dragon under the spell of awakening, Brahim will hold the power. He will control the beast and become the dragon rider.'

'There is no evidence of the existence of dragon riders,' Beatrice said. 'It's in the scriptures only as prophecy.'

'It's a prophecy born from the pattern,' Crandor said. 'A hybrid without understanding of their powers as a mage, or knowledge of their path to dragon form, are vulnerable during transformation. It's a vulnerability easily manipulated by someone intent on securing the power of the dragon for themselves. If Brahim succeeds, Luna will be his slave.'

Eleanor said, 'Whether the prophecy is realised or not, we have to stop Brahim and get to Luna before she fully transforms.'

'As warders of Evren, we should go,' Beatrice quietly said. 'But it will take the strength of three to face down the Rayne Yangsens.' She looked first at Crandor, then Eleanor, who each nodded in turn.

It dawned on me that they were considering coming with us. For all their wisdom, in the face of the journey ahead, I saw only danger.

'I haven't left the temple walls since I was a young man,' Crandor said. 'Until this day, I never thought I would again.'

'The crossing is five days sail,' I said, concerned by how they would fare on rough seas.

Beatrice stretched her arms out in front and said, 'I think my old bones would like to feel the strength of the winds again.'

33. Suni

OUTSIDE THE FAMILIAR TEMPLE WALLS, the warders' confident poise was shaken. Travelling down to the docks by mule and cart, there was a grim expression on all our faces to see up close the effects of Papaver. I was glad to reach the safety of the rafts and see the warders relax: they welcomed and revered by the raft people for their gifts.

As the rafts set sail, we gathered at the edge, watching the docks of Evren retreat into the distance.

With her gaze fixed on the island, Eleanor said, 'I've heard of the damage done by Papaver, of cravings that destroy bodies and minds, of sickness and death and orphans left to beg on the streets. But I've never seen it with my own eyes before today.'

'Perhaps the temple shelters us too much,' Beatrice said.

Eleanor turned to face me. 'I'm sorry to know that your land suffers too.'

With the faces of the dead and dying etched on my mind, I thought of my father, all the times he had ignored me, treated me with disdain, or begged me for coins. Was this desperation driven by cravings for more Papaver? Were the men back home destined to live a life intent only on satisfying cravings?

'There must be a cure,' Zandi said, linking her arm through mine.

'There was once, according to the scrolls,' Beatrice said. 'Long ago, when the islands were still forest, there was an indigenous herb with properties we think could counteract the effects of Papaver.'

'What was the name of the herb?' Zandi asked.

'Blue agave,' Beatrice said. 'It doesn't grow anymore. The forests were destroyed in the Great War. After the war, coal was mined and stone houses built from the trade. Wildlife never recovered.'

'Blue agave,' I said, thinking back to Mata's lessons of herbal lore. I looked at Zandi. 'I've heard that name. On Shendi I think we know it as bitter weed.'

Zandi raised her eyebrows and said, 'Bitter weed grows in the sacred forest.'

'Tell me more about your land,' Eleanor said.

As Zandi and I spoke about Shendi's turbulent past, Beatrice went to stand alone at the edge of a neighbouring raft. Stooped over her walking stick, her frailty was obvious. But as the westerly breeze picked up, blowing back her wispy hair, she inched her feet apart and slowly raised her head to face the sea. Whispering into the breeze, her shoulders straightened and her back slowly uncurled. As the breeze gained the force of wind, Beatrice let go of the walking stick and held her arms out at her sides. She tilted her head back, closed her eyes and splayed her fingers, all the while whispering into the wind. Great gusts billowed through the sails as night fell, but Beatrice remained standing, energised by her gift as Windfinder.

Eleanor and Crandor took shelter in Nisrin's hut, each clutching their amulets as they settled down to sleep. I could only wonder where their dreams would take them. The rest of us dragged mats out onto the deck and settled down under the stars.

Serafay was waiting for me as I drifted. Standing before the wall of mist, I hesitated, wary of returning to the forest on fire. But when I emerged from *Serafay*, I found myself in the mountains.

THE SUN WAS SHINING IN a clear blue sky, but the cool of *Serafay* lingered. I looked out across the valley's grasslands from a well-known path, just below my usual point of crossing between the flat summit and its neighbouring splintering peak. Below me, the path was visible all the way to the foothills. I looked around but could see no sign of Wanda. An eagle was circling over the peaked summit, a herd of mountain goats came charging from the higher slope, but I heard no eagle's cries or stampeding hooves. It was strangely silent.

I climbed the path up to an overhang, with a viewpoint looking out over the adjacent mountain. On the slower slope, a landslide of shale was slipping in a slow wave, but there was no sound of rushing stone. On the cliff-face towering over, snaking cracks were creating fissures in the rock. A shard broke loose, dropping down to the lower slope, adding momentum to the landslide. Still there was silence. Until an eagle's cry pierced the skies. I raised my head to see, but *Serafay* came to claim me.

34. Wanda

THE SUN WAS SHINING, BUT I was gripped by the shadow's cool embrace as I trekked across the grasslands, heading for the mountains. I kept my determined gaze fixed on the point of crossing: the flat-topped summit watched over by its neighbouring rocky peak. It was the place I feared, the origin of the shadow, but crossing the mountains was my only way north to Luna.

Hiking over foothills, with the shadow's song ringing in my ears, I kept my jaw clenched and eyes focused on the way ahead. Reaching the mountain pass where the climb grew quickly steep, the shadow fell quiet. The higher I climbed, there was another sound in the air: distant rumbling like thunder. I had lost track of the seasons and looked up, wondering if the rains were coming, but the sky was clear. The rumbling faded, but when I reached higher ground it came again, accompanied by a tremor beneath my feet. I looked down, afraid of what was stirring in the mountains.

For the first time in days, the shadow let go of its tight hold on me, and drifted out in front. I was used to it following my lead, but now it was me who was following, on a steep climb to the summit. I had only ever seen the shadow walking upright, but the higher we climbed, it stooped, as though crawling along the ground. Every so often it stopped, bending even lower, as though peering down into natural fissures in the mountain. I wondered if it might slide back down into the dark recesses from where it came and rid me of its curse, but it didn't. It slithered on ahead over rock and stone, finally disappearing up over the edge of the summit.

I climbed after it, reaching flat ground, before sudden tremors shook the mountain. A crack split the ground, snaking a trail around a jagged edge of rock that slowly broke free, dropping with a dull thud down the mountainside. When the rumbling tremors slowly calmed, I looked up at the towering peak in trepidation of another quake. In the days of the mines there had been two tall peaks side by side, until the earthquakes reshaped the mountains. This time, no more tremors followed.

A sudden cry pierced the sky; the note was low and off pitch, but I recognised the call of a hungry eaglet. An adult eagle came flying overhead, carrying a hare in its talons, on course for the nest on a rocky ledge mid-way up the peak. It wasn't a bird I had encountered before. It was male, judging by its size; the larger female would be somewhere close by. I paused, considering how long it might take to cross the desert on foot, compared to flying with the strength of an eagle's wing. I reached out with my mind, catching the eagle off guard, as it focused on its nest and the hare caught in its talons. I reached further, felt the breadth of its wingspan gliding on the current. Then we began to dive.

'I mean you no harm,' I said to the eagle.

'Sorcerer,' it said, flapping its wings, losing its grip on the hare as it tried to shake free of my presence. 'Who are you that speaks my tongue?'

'I need your help,' I said, pushing back against the resistance. I felt the reach of its claws and tips of its wing feathers as I pushed further than I had gone before, until the eagle's will was forced into the far recesses and I was in control. The heart stopped pounding as I stretched out the wings, catching the current. I glided out of the dive, and beat down with the wings, gaining height as I headed north.

Through the eagle's eyes, the colours of the world appeared bright and sharp: deep green thorn bushes contrasted with the bronze mountain slope; grey foxes moved through yellow-tipped mountain grasses; even brown hare, ordinarily well camouflaged, could not hide from an eagle's sight. Across the mountains the landscape turned to sand, broken by intermittent splashes of colour from oases of greenery. I hadn't seen these barren northern lands since I was a young boy.

Guided by the sun, I flew on a direct path north in the direction of town. As I approached, the horizon grew dark. Drawing closer, I realised a huge storm system stretched out over the entire town, with streaks of lightning flashing through thick grey swirling cloud. I thought of the storm Luna had brought over the cottage, and the dream, seeing her consumed by flames in a forest on fire, as I flew like an arrow into the blanket of grey.

Over farmlands and wide avenues edging the town, swirling winds fanned the flames of burning homes. A sound carried in the gusting air, clicking, humming and screeching like the shadow's song. But I had left the shadow behind. This melody came from every direction, sounding like a random chatter of scattered notes. But deeper into the town where the streets narrowed and the wind blew stronger, the notes came together with the song of Orag. In places it was a sweet melody, in others it sounded with a rasping growl. I battled against the winds, searching for the source of the song, disorientated by random flashes of lightening that kept forcing me off course.

Lost and confused, I looked up. Pushing the eagle's wings down hard on the downstroke, folding them in close on the upwards stroke, I pushed back against swirling currents, flying up and out into blue skies. There was a moment of quiet calm as I soared up high, then I arched into a circling flight, looking down at the swirling mass of frothing cloud rotating around a black centre. I took aim, tucked the wings in tight, and dove down into the eye of the storm.

The song of Orag rang loudly in thick black cloud that gave the appearance of dusk. Sucked in by swirling winds, I was dragged over collapsed, burnt-out buildings and slammed into a rooftop. I hunkered down and looked out, dazed, over the surrounding walled courtyard. Luna was there, tied to a tree by rope wrapped around her middle. Three mysterious strangers surrounded her, two men and a woman, white like the woman in my vision. But it was what lurked in the background behind the tree that caught my attention: a shadow like the one bound to me, only this one was at least five times the size. Its bulging black mass loomed over all, moving with interchangeable forms as screeching, humming and clicking rang out from its dark depths, singing the song of Orag.

The strangers were chanting, heads lowered, as they moved in a circle around Luna, oblivious or unafraid of the shadow they brushed past. Luna was slumped forwards; with hair hanging down over her face, I couldn't tell whether she was even alive. Helpless in eagle form, I cried out, my voice sounding with a high, weak whistle. As though hearing my cry, Luna slowly raised her head, turning to look in my direction with pitch black eyes. She appeared more like a creature than a girl. The rich brown of her skin had faded to cracked grey, the scar on her cheek glowed fiery orange, and when she opened her mouth, two long sharp canines looked like fangs. It was like my dream foretold; my cousin was gone. My heart sank with the thought that I had failed her.

'I see you,' she hissed. 'I'm not weak, like you. I'm not afraid of the thing you fear.'

I felt her lifeless gaze see through my disguise, penetrating the well of cold filling my insides. I pushed my beak open, reaching for the eagle's cry, but the voice was lost. I tried to clench my talons and lift a wing but the body I was housed in was numb to my touch. I watched, helpless, as the strangers stopped chanting, and one man stepped forward to face Luna.

'You are the Chosen One,' he said in a commanding voice. 'And I am Brahim, your master.'

Luna cocked her head, growling as she fixed him in a stare.

She pushed against the ropes and hissed, 'I have no master.'

The shadow closed in behind them, casting its dark silhouette in a wide arc around the tree. The wind blew stronger, howling with the shadow's song.

'I am Brahim,' he called out over the shadow's song. 'Hear my voice and know that I command you!'

He punched a fist high in the air. In turn, a bolt of lightning flashed low over the tree, lighting a spark in the branches. Fire burned down to a broad bough, a smouldering gash streaked down, splitting the bark, searing through the rope binding Luna. As the rope singed and frayed,

Luna hissed and writhed breaking free of the bonds. She stepped forward, fixing Brahim in a deathly stare as behind them the tree burned.

Brahim reached out, pressing a hand against Luna's forehead. Luna leaned forward, pushing against him, forcing Brahim back as she walked towards him with shuffling steps.

'*Sarayon, sarayon, taroah,*' Brahim said. Luna growled, as she tried to take another step, but it was as though his words were holding her. The other two strangers moved in behind Brahim, each placing a hand on his shoulders. '*Sarayon, sarayon, taroah,*' they said together.

Luna hissed and snarled, flaying her arms, though her feet seemed caught or bound in some way. The shadow moved in closer behind her, slowly shrinking in size. It suddenly contracted, collapsing in on itself like a swirling black ball, before a gushing stream of black spewed out and up, arching high overhead. Four more streams came pouring down from the centre. Towering over them, it appeared like a giant headless creature on four legs.

Brahim pressed both hands against Luna's forehead, as he called out, '*Sarayon, sarayon, taroah!*' When he let go with one hand, raising it into the air, the other two strangers backed away towards the building. Brahim looked up into the mass of shadow and shouted out, '*Baracol scincyrin!*'

The body of the shadow bulged, pushing out what appeared to be a featureless head at the end of a long neck. The neck came swooping down, followed by the legs retracting behind it, joining the stream of black cascading down and round, coiling around Brahim and Luna like a snake wraps around its prey. Lightning streaked the sky as the wind roared with the shadow's song.

'Transform,' Brahim's booming voice echoed out from behind the spinning wall of black. 'Know that I command you! Become the dragon and know me as your rider! *Baracol scincyin!*'

Then the world fell silent and I was floating in a pitch-black sky.

35. Suni

IN THE EARLY HOURS OF sunrise, the rafts anchored in the coastal waters of Shendi. Out at sea the sky was ablaze with the colours of dawn, but over land the horizon was dark. The storm over Shendi had gone, and in its place, an unworldly black stain like pooling ink stretched out over the town.

'What is that?' Nisrin said, voicing all our thoughts as we looked out at the unnatural sky.

'The transformation has begun,' Crandor said. 'We can only hope we are not too late.'

The strained look on his face, compounded my existing doubts that he was too frail to match what was coming. But when I looked at Beatrice, I was reminded of the mysterious powers of the warders. Her eyes appeared to sparkle, her face was flushed and her posture straight and tall, as though invigorated by days spent using her gift as windfinder.

Eleanor put her hand on my shoulder, a knowing look in her eyes as she said, 'Now is the time for courage.'

I nodded, reassured by the confidence I saw in her steady gaze.

Nisrin was loosening the mooring ropes of two canoes. Seeing her start to climb down off the deck, I went and took her by the hand.

'You should wait here, Nisrin', I said. 'You've done enough, and we can handle the boats. There's no sense in us all going.' She frowned as she met my gaze.

'Suni's right,' Eleanor said. 'There won't be anything you can do.'

Nisrin hesitated, before she put her hands on my shoulders, drawing me into her embrace.

'The rafts will be here when this is over,' she said, squeezing tight. 'Be careful.'

I turned to Zandi and paused.

'Not likely,' she said, reading my mind. 'I'm coming with you.'

We were a quiet crew as Zandi and I paddled the warders to shore, watched by keepers gathered along the banks of the estuary. Tired anxiety lined all their faces, which sagged into distrust when they realised we had brought strangers.

Chad came forward to help drag the canoes up onto the bank. 'The townspeople have fled to the farms,' he said. 'We'd have run to the valley if we'd known what was coming. We were stranded out here before we knew what to do.' He paused, casting a suspicious glance at the warders.

I climbed out of the boat, helping Beatrice out after. 'Our guests are warders of the temple,' I said, meeting Chad's eye. 'They've come to help.'

Alanda stepped forward. 'It didn't work out well the last time we welcomed strangers here.'

'We've been deceived by imposters,' I said. 'These are true warders, with powers to match the damage done by the Rayne Yangsens. They are our only hope now.'

The keepers slowly moved aside as Zandi and I led the way up the bank, but Chad went to follow.

Eleanor turned to him and said, 'Your bows and arrows are no use to us.'

'The priestess is right,' Zandi said. 'You should all wait here.'

There was disquiet among the keepers as we left the shores and headed into town.

Beneath a pitch-black sky, a cool breeze swept through darkened streets, filling the air with drifting ash from burnt-out buildings. A song carried in the breeze, like the song sung over the Dragon Lands, humming notes rising and falling in waves, forming the word of Orag in its melody. The song grew louder the closer we came to the old school, echoing through abandoned streets, blowing all around in the blustery air until it was ringing in my ears. The warders went ahead, holding hands as they chanted, but the sound of their voices was soon drowned out by the dragon's song. My heart started pounding in my chest, my stomach turned with sudden nausea, and a lump formed in my throat as a wave of unexplained sadness washed over me. When Zandi grabbed my hand, I saw my own despair reflected in her face. Overwhelmed, we both stopped, clinging to one another.

'What's happening?' she said.

'I don't know, but we've got to keep moving.'

With arms wrapped around each other's waists, we pushed on to the school, crouching down in a pile of rubble next to the fallen school gate. In the middle of the devastated yard, the building was still standing, aside from one collapsed edge. Two figures were huddled together, covered in dust as they sat crouched against the school wall. It was Ray and Adela, looking straight ahead with vacant, staring eyes. At first, I thought they were both dead, but subtle movements told me they were alive, frozen in fear or madness.

Next to the smouldering stump that had once been the palm tree, the warders were standing in a circle, holding hands, heads back to face the sky as they chanted words of the old tongue. Overhead, the sky was stirring. This had been the eye of the storm; now it looked like a whirlpool slowly rousing in the black-stained sky, swirling faster as the warders chanted louder. And all the while the song of Orag reigned down, growing higher in pitch, until a deafening shriek rang out.

The circle of warders broke. Beatrice raised her arms in the air, reaching with fingers splayed as she stretched up high. Crandor and Eleanor moved in behind her, laying their hands on her shoulders, leaning in as though they were taking strain.

'*Verinee veratum valoh!*' Beatrice called out, her voice booming with a supernatural, resounding echo into the screeching wind.

Overhead, as though by the power of Beatrice's command, the swirling black sky spun faster into a maelstrom that funnelled down, forming a stream of black that broke free of the pooling sky. As it dove down, Beatrice squatted down then pushed back up, her voice roaring into the wind:

'*Verinee veratum valoh! Sarayon, sarayon, taroah!*'

The black stream slowed into a gathering mass that hovered high above the warders' heads. The dragon song fell quiet until it was just a background lull in the calming winds. The bulging mass shifted and formed, slowly revealing the silhouette of the dragon within: two wings sprouted; a horned tail pushed out, followed by legs tipped with clawed feet; and finally, a long neck uncoiled, swooping down with an arrow-shaped head, staring down at the warders with eyes of fiery orbs, in shining contrast to the jet-black body.

Eleanor and Crandor kept their hands gripped on Beatrice's shoulders, as, with arms still raised, she bent forwards, turning from side to side, whispering into the wind. All around her, sand stirred on the dusty ground, sweeping low then rising high in clouds that settled below the shadowy dragon. The dragon beat its wings, writhing as it shrieked wildly. But when Beatrice lowered her arms, it was as though her powers tamed the dragon. The creature fell quiet as it was brought down to rest on the ground.

Eleanor and Crandor quietly chanted: '*Sarayon, sarayon, taroah!*', while Beatrice lowered her head as though bowing to the creature. In turn, the dragon folded its wings, dipped its head to the side, coiling its neck round until its snout reached the tip of its tail. It started to spin, slow at first, then fast, until its shape was lost in a swirling black cloud. When Beatrice joined the chanting, the cloud faded to grey, revealing two figures inside. Luna was sitting cross-legged on the ground, with her head bent low, hair hanging down over her face. Brahim was standing over her, looking out at the warders with glowing orange eyes.

Crandor broke from chanting and called out, 'Luna, remember yourself. Remember who you are.'

Luna didn't look up when Brahim said, 'The girl is mine!'

'*Verinee veratum valoh!*' Crandor said, stepping to Beatrice's side. 'Luna, Brahim wants to control you. He wants the power of the dragon. Remember yourself.' He reached a hand out towards them. '*Sarayon, sarayon, taroah!*'

An unworldly shriek suddenly rang out in the air all around, splintering stone as cracks formed in surrounding walls. All three warders stepped forward, circling Brahim and Luna as they chanted:

'*Verinee veratum valoh, verinee veratum valoh,* s*arayon, sarayon, taroah.*'

'You're too late,' Brahim said, with eyes glowing like fire as he raised his arms out at his sides. 'The power of the dragon is mine.' He thrust his hands out towards Eleanor and Crandor, opened his mouth and yelled, 'Yah!'

Lightning poured from his mouth and hands, gushing towards each of the warders. They pushed back, leaning in with arms outstretched, repelling Brahim's attack with splayed hands. Fighting back against the power of the dragon, the strain took its toll. Eleanor was the first to fall to her knees, then Crandor; both slumped forward with their energy spent. But Beatrice stayed standing.

I thought she would fight, or fall, but she did neither. She lowered her arms, allowing lightning to stream into her face. Caught in the surge of Brahim's power, she was silent as her whole body shook. I was sure it would kill her, but instead she changed. The transformation happened in moments, before our eyes: her hair thickened, with grey darkening to fiery orange; and she grew several feet taller, with a strong, youthful posture. She swung her arms forward, effortlessly pushing back against Brahim's power, as she walked towards him. For a moment, Brahim looked shocked. Then he lowered his arms, ceasing his attack, fear on his face as he watched her advance. Beatrice paused, briefly lowering her arms, before she pushed forward with her hands, sending a sudden storm of lightning pouring out over Brahim. He tried to push back but his arms buckled, sending raw power streaming in all directions. Eleanor and Crandor pinned themselves flat to the ground. I ducked down with Zandi as lightning flashed low over our heads. But Adela and Ray had remained paralysed throughout. They shared Brahim's fate, burning in the power of the dragon.

36. Suni

THE AIR FELL SILENT AND still, sand settling on the ground. I looked out from the rubble, wiped dust from my eyes, and squinted in bright sunlight to see the shadowy dragon was gone. I cupped a hand over my brow and looked up. Like a pot cracked by fire, shards of sunlight shone through the black-stained sky. A lump formed in my throat to think the curse was finally lifting.

Zandi slowly stood and reached for my hand. We clambered over the rubble and across what was left of the yard. The charred bodies of the Rayne Yangsens were a gruesome sight, with wisps of smoke still drifting from their burnt-out eyes. It was a relief to see the warders stirring, slowly rising up onto their hands and knees, crawling forwards to sit closer to where Luna lay curled on the ground. I went to her, kneeling among the warders, reality weighing heavy when I saw up close how Luna had changed. Her lips were parted revealing two elongated fangs; the scar on her cheek now covered one side of her face, and was leathery and textured like scales; the same leathery skin covered one of her hands, with fingernails long and pointed like claws; and two bony protrusions had broken through the skin of her forehead. I watched the gentle rise and fall of her chest, tears welling in my eyes as I thought of her future as a hybrid. She had been robbed of her life, her freedom. How to tell a mother that her daughter would never grow to be a woman?

'Luna is powerful,' Beatrice said.

She appeared as an old woman once more. All the warders looked drained by the ordeal.

'Whatever power she has,' I said, 'it has cursed her.'

'When did she get the scar on her cheek?' Crandor asked.

'When she was a baby,' I said. 'She was burnt by a fire in the mountains.'

The warders quietly looked at one another, before Beatrice said, 'Then Luna is *Maravin*; touched by the dragon. The fire that burned her as a baby was no ordinary fire, it was the breath of Evren.' She paused, eyes downcast. 'It explains why someone so young possesses the power of a mage.'

'What will happen to her now?' Zandi asked.

Beatrice kept her eyes on Luna. 'This could be the closest we've come to understanding the form Evren takes.' She paused then said, 'But the girl is weak. There is no telling whether she has the strength to survive.'

It was the first time I had considered the possibility that Luna might not be saved.

'We will do what we can to prevent further transformation,' Beatrice said. She turned to Crandor sitting across from her. When their gaze met, they nodded, each holding their hands out above Luna's chest, speaking in low voices: '*Holav mutarev eenirev.*'

I turned to Eleanor but she was gazing intently out to the side. She didn't speak when she stood up and walked over to the school. I went to her, following her gaze up to the roof, where an eagle lay slumped on the tiles.

Zandi came up behind me and put a hand on my shoulder. 'What's an eagle doing this far from the mountains?' she said.

Eleanor slowly turned to look at us with hope in her eyes. 'There's another warder here.'

I watched, bemused, as she untied the cape from around her neck and wrapped it round her forearm. She raised her bound arm up, calling out to the eagle in words of the old tongue. The eagle shifted its wings and slowly lifted its head, dragging itself to the edge. It made a weak attempt to flap its wings as it fell, landing heavily on Eleanor's arm.

'You have the gift with animals,' I said.

'Not me,' Eleanor said. 'A gifted boy flies with this bird. Someone close to Luna.'

I stared in disbelief but she kept her eyes on the eagle, smoothing down its ruffled feathers.

'Is that possible?' I said. When the eagle's beady eyes met mine, I thought back to the strangeness of my recent dreams, trying to order my confused thoughts.

'Tell me who it is,' Eleanor said, watching me closely.

I thought of the dream, seeing Wanda at the cave, looking out over the valley with only the whites of his eyes showing.

'Luna's cousin, Wanda. He is gifted with animals.' I shook my head, but I knew, somehow, it was true.

'Wanda,' Eleanor said to herself. Her gaze slowly drifted back to the eagle. 'His gift with animals is more powerful than any I've heard of. He has learnt to see through a creature's eyes, but he has stayed too long.'

'How is this possible?' I asked.

'I don't know. But he came here in search of Luna, because he is her warder.' She turned to face me. 'We need to find him and return him to his body. Wanda is the best chance Luna has got.'

'He's in the mountains,' I said, believing in the power of my dreams.

BEATRICE AND CRANDOR STAYED BEHIND to watch over Luna, holding her in a dreamless sleep with their continuous stream of melodious chanting. The rest of us set off for the mountains, carrying the eagle safely in a crate since it was too weak to fly.

Two black mares carried us across the desert plains, south west to the foothills of the flat-topped mountain, with Eleanor riding behind Zandi, holding the eagle in its box between them. Traversing the foothills, the sound of distant rumbling carried in the air. The mountain slopes we were heading for appeared calm, but in the high slopes of mountains either side, clouds of dust gathered over slow-moving landslips of shale. Arriving at the mountain path, setting out on a steep ascent, we began the climb with trepidation, but the ground remained still. As we reached the higher slopes, it was the eagle that began to stir. It appeared dazed when Eleanor lifted it out, perching it on her arm, whispering into its ear. Whether revitalised by fresh mountain air or the sound of Eleanor's voice, as she swooped her arm forward it ruffled its feathers and spread its wings, catching the current. The eagle's whistling cries rang out as it plateaued in a wide arc before gaining height, soaring up to its nest perched in a high crag of the neighbouring peak.

It was evening by the time we reached the summit. I led the way over levelled ground in the direction of the path that had featured in my dream. Seeing Wanda up ahead, sprawled out on his back, I jumped down from the horse and ran to him. In the light of the full moon, his rich brown skin looked sickly pale, his cheeks were hollow, his lips dry and cracked, and dark shadows framed his closed eyes. I knelt beside him, laying a hand on his chest to feel the gentle rise and fall of his breaths, as I leaned over and kissed his face.

37. Wanda

DRIFTING AMONG STARS IN A night sky, I thought I must have died. There was no sense of space or time, just random memories of people and places I had known, memories of myself as a child and as a young man, of a shadow, a hawk, and an eagle. Memories were fleeting in these vast skies where only my mind existed.

'*Sarayon, sarayon, taroah. Owar, sarayon, sarayon, taroah.*'

The whispering voice was out of place, but I understood the meaning; my gift had always recognised the old tongue. The soothing voice was beckoning, calling to the 'warder'. I wondered if other minds were floating in the night sky, since it was not a name I had heard before. I listened, curious to know the origin of the voice, and found myself drifting towards a bright star. Gazing at the radiating glow of light, I watched the brightness slowly fade and colours begin to form.

'Wanda.'

I recognised Suni's voice. When she called my name again, I felt her breath on my face. I opened my eyes and saw her looking down at me.

'I saw you,' I whispered, struggling to form words with my dry mouth. 'I saw you in my dream.'

A tear fell from her eye and landed on my cheek. She nodded and smiled, then moved back out of my eyeline, leaving me looking at the dusky sky. I tilted my head to find her, and saw that Zandi was there too, and another woman I didn't recognise: a stranger with pale white skin. I tried to sit up, thinking of the strangers attacking Luna with their powerful words. '*Baracol sincyrin.*' The spell still echoed in my mind.

141

'Ssh,' Suni said, putting her hands on my shoulders and gently guiding me to lie back down. 'Just relax.'

'Luna,' I said, my voice croaking, panic rising in my chest.

'Luna is safe,' Suni said, smoothing a hand across my brow. 'This is Eleanor. She's a friend, and she's going to help you.'

I looked back at the woman, wary despite Suni's reassurance. Caught in the gaze of her piercing blue eyes, absorbed by the subtle flecks of grey, wariness turned to intrigue, as I thought of the woman, Evren, in my vision. They had the same striking eyes and youthful complexion, but this woman's hair was bleached white as though with age. When the shadow drifted into view, lurking over the woman's shoulder, I turned my gaze back to the sky.

Quiet moments passed until Eleanor said, 'I know what you fear.' There was kindness in her voice, the same voice that had beckoned me while drifting among the stars. 'I can help you.'

I looked back at her, keeping my eyes fixed on hers, despite the shadow blurring the edges. Seized by the compassion I saw in her gaze, I suddenly felt naked before her. I was afraid she would see my hidden secrets, but felt compelled by her mystery. In that moment I thought she was the most beautiful woman I had ever seen.

'All your unanswered questions, all the invisible bonds you have felt tugging at your heart, lie in the truth of who you are, a warder, like me.' She paused as her gaze flicked to the side, towards where the shadow lurked. When her eyes turned back on me, her lips were still but I heard her gentle voice inside my head: *'There are others who see shadows. Be in no doubt that your heart is good.'*

A lump formed in my throat as I stared at her for a quiet moment, trying to make sense of her powers.

Finally, I asked, 'What is a warder?'

'There is time for your questions but first you must eat. You've grown weak.'

Suni helped me to sit up then passed me a flask of water. In-between long sips my eyes met hers, as I thought of her presence in the forest dream. She was gifted, but just how much did she know? Killing the hawk with my own hands had been just a dream, but eating the raw flesh of a hare was not. But Suni's gentle smile did not falter. I rested my head against her shoulder, eating soft crusts of bread, watching Zandi coax a fire to light. As the fire took hold and the eagle cried out from its nest, in that moment I decided I would never again venture to see the world through any eyes except my own. Surrounded by the kindness of friends, I felt safer than I had done in years.

Suni sat back, cupping my face in her hands. 'I want you to talk to Eleanor.' She held my gaze then softly smiled. 'Secrets are a burden.'

She stood up and went with Zandi to sit on an overhang looking out over the valley, leaving us alone.

Moments of quiet passed before Eleanor said, 'Tell me about the shadow bound to you.'

'Do you see it?' I whispered, taken aback.

'No, but I see the feelings it evokes in you. The shadow is corrupt and sees your gift. Tell me how you came to know it.'

I stared into space, taking a long reminiscent sigh, then, for the first time, I spoke about the shadow:

'My dreams led me to it when I was a child, dreams about the mines in these mountains.'

'Were you a miner?'

'I was only five years old, but yes, I worked in the mines as a child, until Suni got me out.'

'Go on.'

'So much changed after we escaped the mines. Then the dreams came.' I paused, then resumed. 'The mines were different in my dreams: the tunnels were deserted. It was the same dream every night: I was alone, roaming the tunnels, but I had the feeling I was being watched. Then one night a voice whispered in the dark, speaking its name, Orag; it was the name of an evil spirit that had attacked us before.' I rubbed my clammy hands against my legs, aware of the shadow moving in front of me. I kept my eyes on Eleanor, reassured to see no change in her calm expression. 'After that, the voice returned every night in my dreams. Each morning I would wake covered in sweat, terrified at the thought of what was speaking to me. Why me?' I paused, taking a long slow breath. 'Then I started hearing it when I was awake. Sometimes it was quiet and distant, other times it was louder like it was close. It was like it was calling to me, wanting me to find it. And one day I followed, all the way up into the mountains.'

'How old were you then?' she said.

'About eight.'

Eleanor gently shook her head. 'You were so young.'

'I was scared but I was also curious. It was sunset by the time I stopped in the shade of an overhang, where the voice of Orag was ringing so loud, it echoed all around.'

I paused, hearing clicking, humming and screeching quietly drifting out of the shadow. Eleanor's gaze flicked to the side.

'Can you hear it?' I asked.

She nodded. 'Keep going.'

My heart was beating faster as I continued, 'The ground at my feet turned black. It was like the dark silhouette of a man forming in the shadow cast from the overhang. The man-shaped shadow rose up from the ground to stand before me. When it reached out to touch me, I should have run but I was too frightened to move.' I brushed a hand over my forearm. 'Evil attached itself to me that day. I've been cursed by its song and its cool touch ever since.'

Eleanor gazed intently into my eyes.

'You cannot know that the shadow is evil,' she said. 'In any case, it is not your fault that it was let loose.' I swallowed the lump in my throat as I stared at her, clinging to the understanding I saw there. 'And the fact it bound itself to you, is not a reflection of you or your character.'

'How do you know?' I asked, feeling lighter with every word spoken.

'Because I know of your gift to speak the tongue of animals. It's the reason you heard the voice, the reason it had the power to influence you.' She softly smiled. 'But you also have another gift, the gift of a warder. I can help you understand your true nature, since it is a gift I share.'

I held onto the sincerity in her eyes. This strange, beautiful woman saw all that I was, but she didn't turn away. I dared to feel hope. But my shadow wasn't the only shadow.

'What about Luna?' I said. 'I saw another shadow and it has her.'

'We found Luna. She is safe in the care of my fellow warders, for now. But she's going to need you.'

When she moved closer to the fire, I followed. Warmed by the flames, I learned of Eleanor's distant homeland, a place with hybrids and dragons. All the extraordinary things I had witnessed, all the fear of losing my mind, began to make sense. My gift with animals had enabled my connection to the dragon in the mountains, a connection manifested in the shadow. All this time the dragon had been speaking the spell of Orag, tempting me in its desire to wake. The woman I had seen was Evren before the dragon, and the eye of flames, showing me the islands burning, were Evren's memories. Eleanor listened, intrigued, as I told of my visions.

'Of all the dragons, Evren has always been a mystery to us,' she said. 'You are the only one alive who has seen her.'

'I saw a woman, but as for what carried me to the islands, it wasn't clear to see.' I paused, then said, 'But I'm not the only one to see her. Luna saw her too, as a woman in my shadow.'

Eleanor nodded, eyes gently narrowed in a thoughtful gaze. 'You are close to Luna.'

'We have always been close, but the last few days we spent together, it was more than that. I don't know how to explain it.' I glanced down at the ground, nervously fiddling with my fingers. 'I saw her, with those people in town. I saw her changed.' I looked back up at Eleanor. 'What's happening to my cousin?'

'Luna is *Maravin*,' she said. 'Touched by the dragon. And you are her warder. It is the strength of the warder's bond you felt. I share the same bond with my father. He's a hybrid, a transcender, like Luna. I have been his warder throughout, working to prevent full transformation to the dragon. You will do the same for Luna.'

I looked away, staring into space, trying to absorb the immensity of what she was saying. How could I believe that my cousin was part dragon? Yet I had witnessed the storm and seen her hybrid features start to form. She was powerful and lost, but somewhere deep down she was still the same girl.

'Why is this happening? Why Luna?' I leaned forward, resting my elbows on my knees. 'I should never have left her.'

'The gifts fall where they fall,' Eleanor said. 'But in Luna's case, it's a tragedy, and for that I am sorry. No infant should face the powers of a dragon.' She paused, then said, 'But we can do nothing to change the past. As her warder, it is up to you to forge your connection for the future.' She leaned in closer. 'Tell me about times you spent with Luna. Tell me a happy memory.'

I gazed into space as I recalled nights spent camping in the forest with Luna, and days exploring wildlife on old and new pathways; memories that had found their way into my dreams.

'Then the forest is the place of your shared dream,' Eleanor said. 'The dream I share with my father is of the cliffs, exploring the caves and rock pools like we did when I was a girl. Shared dreams are the key for your gift as a warder; they are the place you can meet, where you will work to keep Luna safe.'

'But it's not safe in the dream,' I said, pulling my knees up and hugging them into my chest. 'Changes happen in the forest, small things at first, but then the whole place fills with smoke. The last time I saw Luna there, she was on fire and the whole forest burned.'

'Fire came from the dragon,' Eleanor said. She picked up a twig, poking it into the embers, stoking the flames. 'You must understand, Luna is not just a girl, she is also a dragon. In the waking world she's a hybrid, with the dragon half now more powerful than the girl. But in the dream, they are separate.' She dropped the stick into the fire and turned to face me. 'Even in a dragon fully transformed, the human still exists in the dream, since the dream reflects what is now and what is past. In your shared dream with Luna, the girl is there and the dragon is there. As her warder, it is up to you to keep the girl half strong, to keep her from sensing the dragon.'

'But how? When smoke comes, I lose her.'

'Because smoke is a sign that the dragon is close,' she said. 'These signs will frighten and confuse her, and the more she senses the dragon, the more power the dragon has. It is up to you to keep her attention away from the dragon, to keep her content and believing that the dream world is the waking world. This is how you keep the dragon at bay.'

'And how do I keep her from sensing the dragon?'

'You start by understanding the dream,' she said. 'Your role is to keep the girl strong. Therefore, to the dragon, you are the enemy. It wants to assume power over the girl, and wants to be rid of your influence. Fire and smoke are common tricks that prey on your fears, confuse and disorientate you, to separate you from Luna.' She pulled the shawl tighter around her shoulders. 'You must control your fear and know that, although you might lose Luna, you will always find her again. Even in a dragon fully transcended, the human will always exist in the dream since it was once human. For a transcender in the early stages, like Luna, the human form is strong. Luna wants you to find her.'

'But I do find her,' I said. 'And then she runs away.'

'She's not running from you, she's running from the dragon. Like I said, you must keep her from sensing the dragon.'

'But how?' I said. 'I can't control the dream.'

'Yes you can, since it is also your dream. Your gift as a warder means you have the power to create change in the dream world. Smoke is an illusion brought by the dragon, to confuse you, and to make Luna question her reality; then she will wake. The dragon wants her to wake, since then it has power over her.' She paused, fixing her gaze on me as she let her words sink in. 'See through the illusions, remember the forest as it should be, and that is what you will create. By maintaining the truth of the dream and keeping the forest as it should be, Luna will remain content. She won't remember the dragon, and she won't realise that it is a dream. She will believe that the dream world is the waking world, and there will be no further change to her hybrid form.'

'But how do I keep the forest as it should be? If something changes, how can I change it back?'

'Stay alert to the changes, however small, and believe in your ability to change them back to your true memory. We call it laying wards. If sounds are distorted, choose to hear them as you know they should sound. If a colour is the wrong shade, choose to see it as it should look. If a path veers the wrong way, choose to remember the right direction.'

She leaned in closer. 'By remembering the truth, you have the power to create change; you just have to believe in that power.'

I gripped my knees tighter to my chest and looked out across the moonlit mountains. I had been lost in the world. Now I was found by a woman from distant shores, whose presence made me feel stronger. I didn't want to be alone again. Alone, I didn't believe I had the strength to protect my cousin. I glanced at the shadow lurking by the fire. Alone, I didn't believe I had the strength to protect myself.

'You don't have to be alone anymore.' I looked at Eleanor, wondering about her powers that could read my thoughts.

'I don't want to be alone,' I said. 'I can't do this on my own.'

'None of us can. Warders find strength in each other, and the temple walls offer protection for those transcending. You and Luna are my people now, and the temple can be your home.'

38. Suni

IN THE COOL LIGHT OF morning, we rode north across the desert back towards town. With Wanda quietly riding behind me, I could only wonder where his thoughts took him. The valley was all he had known since being a young boy.

My heart felt heavy with the thought of him leaving. I wanted to believe I could help him, watch over him as I had done when he was a child, but I had no place in the dream he shared with Luna. The time for Wanda belonging to the valley had passed; he looked to Eleanor now.

Since Wanda and the priestess had met, he appeared as though a weight had been lifted from his shoulders. I smiled to think of the sparkle in his eye, and the flush of colour in both their cheeks when their gaze lingered. Whatever doubts I had about the future, I suspected Wanda might soon come to know love as a man. I trusted he would be safe in Eleanor's hands. I had always known him as a boy with a gift, but only Eleanor understood where that gift had taken him.

The sky over the town was mostly clear, aside from sweeping trails of grey still dissipating where the eye of the storm had been. We dismounted, releasing the horses back into the wild, then approached the farms on foot. Through the lanes between fields, we passed townspeople too afraid to return to what was left of their homes. No one came near. They peered at us with suspicion, likely out of fear of Eleanor, the stranger among us.

Ntombi, Juna and Sunette were camped out among the maize fields with the mule and cart. Juna came down the lane to meet us as we approached.

'Am I glad to see you,' he said, meeting my eye. He glanced briefly at Eleanor, with a subtle nod, then turned to Wanda. 'What are you doing here, lad?' When Wanda didn't answer, Juna gripped his shoulders, pulling him into a fatherly hug.

'We'll explain everything,' I said. 'The others need to hear it too.'

Juna went to put his arm around Wanda, but Wanda side-stepped and sat down at the verge of the field.

'I'll wait here,' he said, casting a wary eye out towards where Ntombi and Sunette were waiting.

Eleanor sat down next to him and looked at me. 'It's probably better if they hear it from you.'

We left them together and went to join Ntombi and Sunette.

As we began to tell them all that had transpired, Ntombi's gaze drifted out towards Wanda. With the tension between the two of them palpable, I wondered if it was regret I saw in Ntombi's eyes. When I spoke about the Rayne Yangsens' corruption, it came as no surprise. That Luna was now a hybrid came as a devastating blow. Silent tears rolled down Ntombi's face, Juna gritted his teeth, strain on his face as he stared straight ahead, but no one said anything in protest. Wanda and Luna were leaving. Only the warders could help them now.

Ntombi and Sunette rode in the cart, as we led the mule through the ruined streets. Arriving at the school, Wanda went ahead, dropping to his knees at the sight of Luna. No words could prepare a family to see their loved one transformed. Luna appeared to be sleeping as we lifted her into the back of the cart, surrounded by sobs for the girl she had been.

AT THE BANKS OF THE estuary, Juna and Ntombi held Luna's hands as they said their quiet goodbyes. Then Juna scooped her into his arms, tears pooling in his eyes as he carried Luna down the bank and laid her out in the canoe. I turned to Wanda and cupped his face in my hands, smiling to see maturity in his eyes.

'We'll be all right,' he said, as I hugged him tight.

'Give them time to settle,' Eleanor said, putting a hand on my shoulder. 'Then you're all welcome to visit.'

Wanda went to walk past the cart, but Ntombi held an arm out to stop him. He paused, looking at her, before accepting her hand.

'I'm sorry I blamed you,' she said.

They shared a quiet exchange, before Wanda said, 'It wasn't your fault.'

Waving the canoes off from the shore, the air felt filled with bittersweet.

39. Wanda

I NEVER IMAGINED I WOULD leave my homeland and sail the seas. But I didn't look back as the rafts set sail. Whatever the future held, mine and Luna's fate were in the warders' hands now.

The raft people kept their distance, as I carried Luna tight to my chest, following Nisrin and Eleanor deep into the fleet of bound rafts. Beatrice and Crandor followed closely behind, still whispering a stream of spells despite their weariness. Luna's hybrid features were bizarre and spoke of untamed powers, but they didn't frighten me. It was what I had seen in the dream, Luna burning, possessed, that made me clutch her so tight my muscles ached. I would do everything in my power to protect her.

I laid Luna down in Nisrin's hut, reassured by the thought our host was Suni's good friend. Thanks to Beatrice and Crandor's efforts, a thin grey haze lingering over Luna's body was all that remained of the shadow that had consumed her. But the warders were exhausted by their efforts. It was up to me now.

'Drink this,' Eleanor said, handing me a vial. 'It will help you sleep.'

I raised the bottle to my lips but paused, glancing at my own shadow lurking close at my side.

Eleanor put her hand on my shoulder. 'I'll be watching over you until we reach the safety of the temple.'

I met her insightful gaze, for the first time believing that the shadow was not my burden alone.

She nodded and said, 'Remember, smoke and fire are just the dragon's illusions. See through them. Work to keep the forest as you remember.'

The confidence I saw in Eleanor's eyes put any remaining doubts to rest. I drank the potion and settled down in the chair, feeling the gentle sway of the rafts as I closed my eyes.

EYES STINGING, BLINDED BY SMOKE, I heard Luna calling my name: 'Wanda!'

She sounded frightened, and close by, but I couldn't see my own hand in front of my face. She called again but I closed my eyes, stilled my thoughts and pictured the forest I knew.

There is no smoke in my dream. There is no smoke in this forest.

'Wanda,' she called again. Now she sounded impatient. 'Where are you?'

I opened my eyes and saw the air was clear.

'Stay where you are, Luna. I'll come to you.'

I followed the sound of her voice, cutting through a copse of elderbirch. The path was familiar, but the forest was oddly quiet. I paused, imagining the deep-throated song of the crimson-bellied warbler, and the high-pitched calls of long-tailed parakeets. I looked up into the low branches of a tree, thinking about the soft chirps of a jayfinch, and saw its enclosed, round nest with a single narrow opening, decorated with the yellow feathers of the mother's belly.

With birdsong emanating through the canopy, I carried on down the path and saw Luna up ahead. I smiled to see her appearing like an ordinary girl.

'I thought I'd lost you,' she said.

'I found a jayfinch nest,' I said. 'Come see.'

Heading back down the path, holding hands with Luna, I paid attention to the sights and sounds of the forest. Somewhere in the undergrowth, a bullfrog called with low guttural croaks that signified the mating season. I listened to the familiar rhythm of three short croaks from the male, then a pause, followed by the rumbling drawn-out note of the answering female. The pauses between calls grew too short, as the blend of notes became confused. But as I focused my thoughts on how it should sound, the regular pattern slowly resumed.

Luna's hand slipped from mine. I turned to see her running away and followed, calling after her, but she kept on running. I slowed, detecting off-pitch notes in the chorus of birdsong. Sepia flowers edging the path were tinged the wrong shade of blue, and smoke was drifting out from the undergrowth, creeping around my feet. Up ahead, Luna was immersed in smoke up to her waist. When she stopped and turned in my direction, I went to her.

'Luna?'

She was frowning, confused, as her hair shone brightly in sunlight dappling through the trees. When the ends of her hair started to smoulder, confusion faded from her eyes. A slow smile spread across her face as a lock of hair caught fire. She splayed her arms out at her sides, tilted back her head, and slowly rose from the ground.

I moved closer, watching flames flicker through her hair, and down over her arms. *Illusion.* I reached out, feeling the fire was cool, and put my hands under her arms. Her body was tense, but when the flames disappeared she slumped forward, falling into my arms. The territorial warning calls of a crested gannet rang through the trees in a familiar pitch, as I laid Luna gently down on the ground and watched over her as she slept.

Luna slowly opened her eyes, looked at me and said, 'What happened?'

'You fell asleep.' I smiled and helped her to her feet. 'Come. I found a jayfinch nest.'

40. Wanda

EACH TIME I WOKE, I felt as if I hadn't slept in days. While no amount of fish stew could satisfy my insatiable appetite, in the brief times Luna woke she mostly pushed food away.

'You're here,' she would say to me, and little else.

I tried to see the truth behind the faraway look in her eyes, but it was like she had a secret she wouldn't tell. She never mentioned her dreams. Whether it was because she didn't remember them, or didn't realise their significance, I didn't know and didn't ask. Seeing her so quiet and distant was unsettling. I wondered if she was sick, or simply missing home. It was only in the forest dream that I saw the girl I knew.

The slow grinding of the rafts brought life at sea to an end. I had imagined the islands to be forested lands, like my vision, but I saw they were much changed. We boarded one of several canoes, with Nisrin and some of the men accompanying us to shore. Luna was dressed in a hooded cloak that mostly concealed her hybrid features; still I held her close, shielding her face with a protective arm as we made our way through the docks.

The raft people arranged for a mule and cart, and escorted us through dark lanes. I was horrified by the sight of dead bodies lying in the street, and shrank back from skeletal men with knives and a dangerous glint in their eye as they considered us. I turned to Eleanor, wondering why she had failed to mention that her homeland was such a foreboding place, but was silenced by the shame I saw in her eyes. With Luna huddled under my arm, I kept the hood pulled down low over her face.

We parted ways with the raft people when we reached the main street, where the faces of dragons looked out from murals all around. I turned away, resting my chin on Luna's head that was nestled against my chest, and contemplated a lifetime resisting the dragon.

'We're almost there,' Eleanor said, in a tone meant to be reassuring.

When we finally stepped inside the temple, watching the last sliver of daylight disappear as the wooden doors closed behind us, I longed for home.

Eleanor came to stand beside me and put a hand on my arm. My stomach stirred with the warmth of her touch.

'It feels strange to you now, but give yourself time,' she said. 'These walls have given sanctuary to people like us for centuries.'

People like us. Since we had first met, I felt the connection between us grow with each moment that passed. Turning to face her, the hint of vulnerability in her eyes cast her in a new light. On the mountains she had guided me back to life, but compared to the power of the temple, I imagined her gift as a mere spark in the temple's fiery glow. She was looking at me as though she needed me like I needed her, as though, together, we would be stronger. In her company, breathing in the mysterious ambience contained within the intriguing walls, the horrors of the docks slowly washed away. The temple housed a world of its own, with sturdy foundations built on the strength and commitment of the gifted. This was where Luna could be safe. This was where we could both belong.

History was retold throughout the hallways, where fire-spitting dragons and forests on fire featured in mosaic designs. In the room we were allocated, with twin beds and sparse but comfortable furnishings, the plain tiles offered a more relaxing atmosphere. I lay Luna down on one of the beds and sat in the armchair beside her. Her glazed expression gave nothing away as she turned onto her side to face the wall.

'The temple will provide whatever you both need,' Eleanor said, looking down at Luna. She paused, coming to stand by my side, and lowered her voice as she continued. 'For the most part, Luna will not see the truth of her reality. This lack of awareness develops naturally in the minds of all our hybrids, and seems to help them find peace with their existence. It will be harder for you, as it is for me with my father.'

I was distracted by the cool touch of the shadow brush against the back of my neck. As I turned to see its dark silhouette creep along the wall, my mouth turned up into a wry smile. No matter the distance travelled, there was no outrunning my curse.

LIKE ALL THE WARDER/HYBRID connections, my explicable bond with Luna was symbolised with a locket worn around our necks, containing a lock of each other's hair. They were amulets, sealed with powerful words to enhance our bond.

Luna spent most of her time in the forest dream. I met her there often, living and reliving our past in endless cycles. During the times she woke, we took short walks through the hallways and out into the yard. She never mentioned my shadow or the grey haze that lingered around her. She never asked for her mother, or about anything of consequence. Now and again she would refer to her surroundings: the warders we passed by, the pictures in the walls, the caw of flocking gulls. They were casual observations to pass the time, spoken with indifference, as though Shendi belonged in a forgotten past and the temple was all there was. Yet the faraway look remained in her eyes. The more time passed, the more eager she was to return to the sanctuary of her room. Soon she refused to leave at all, and remained curled in a ball facing the wall, sleeping nuzzled against it like a child to her mother's breast.

Routine became my sanctuary. Late one afternoon, I took my customary walk out across the cliffs, enjoying the weight of the wood strapped to my back. After a steep climb up the beacon, I emerged by the dwindling fire in time to stoke the flames. I found comfort in the practicalities of this simple daily ritual, and satisfaction in knowing the role the beacon played, saving lives that might otherwise be lost to the Dragon Lands.

Looking out over choppy seas, the cool of the shadow lingered close by. Its song joined the chorus carried in the fresh sea breeze, but I paid it no mind. Just as Eleanor had promised, I felt strengthened by the temple, and emboldened by the knowledge that I wasn't the only one who saw ghostly manifestations. Like twigs stoking a flame, fear fed the shadow. The more I mastered my fears, the more redundant the shadow became.

Distracted by the sound of footsteps slapping against stone steps, I turned and saw Eleanor emerge from the stairwell.

'I thought I'd find you here,' she said.

I felt giddy with the sudden flutter in my stomach, and pursed my lips to hide my smile. She often sought me out for no reason.

She took her time warming her hands by the fire, then came to stand beside me. Looking out over the seascape, I felt the warmth between us as our arms touched.

'I'm glad you're here,' she said. I turned to face her, but she kept watch over the sea. 'I have my father, and the other warders, but I've felt alone for so long.'

Feeling her hand slide into mine, my cheeks flushed with heat. I brushed my thumb over her fingers, savouring the feel of her soft skin.

'You don't have to be alone anymore,' I said.

Her eyes met mine as she turned to face me, reaching up and brushing her fingers through my hair now streaked with grey. My heart was racing as she leaned in. Feeling her gentle breath on my face, I tilted my head, softly brushing my lips against hers. Absorbed in her arms, time melted away, and as evening fell, with our bodies entwined, we discovered love.

41. Suni

FOR AS LONG AS I could remember, the townspeople had been fractured. Now, after facing a common enemy that no one could deny, new alliances had been forged as people rallied together to rebuild their town. We were more united than we had ever been. All except the outcasts. I hadn't seen my father since before the storm.

After the death of the Rayne Yangsens, Papaver soon ran dry on the streets and the outcasts' condition had taken a rapid decline. Having seen so many dead and dying at the docks of Evren, we temporarily closed our shores to all but the rafts, and set to work collecting bitter weed from the forest. Together with Sunette and Sisile's help, we had perfected a potion to relieve the side effects of Papaver withdrawal. It was handed out freely to anyone wanting to be rid of their cravings, and many men had come forward. But not Fazi.

One evening at dusk, as had become my custom, I stood on the doorstep looking out into the street, hoping my father might come. Our street was among the fortunate ones, mostly untouched by the fires that had claimed many homes. Patsy walked by, greeting me with an awkward smile. No longer adversaries, I smiled back. Watching her turn the corner, I wondered what the future might hold. While some keepers remained in town helping to defend our shores, others had returned to the forest, heading up anti-poaching patrols. That gave me hope for the Mantra, at least.

'Come in,' Zandi said. 'You can't stand there all night.'

I turned to see her at the table, scooping a mound of chopped bitterweed into a box.

'The rafts will soon be here,' I said. I lingered for a moment then stepped inside, closing the door behind me. 'We'll be leaving for the islands whether I've seen Fazi or not.'

Zandi nodded then picked up the box, resting it on her hip. 'I'm just taking this downstairs.' She pulled the tapestry aside, and disappeared down the cellar steps.

I wiped the table and lifted the boiling kettle off the hearth. On my way to the cupboard to fetch mugs, I was stopped by knocking at the door. I paused mid-step, hesitating, before I went and slowly opened the door. Fazi was standing out on the street.

'Can I come in?' he said, when I made no move.

I stepped aside, pleased to see the improvement: the sores on his skin had mostly cleared, and he had filled out, losing the gaunt expression on his face.

Zandi appeared from behind the tapestry. Seeing Fazi, she said, 'I'll make a start downstairs and leave you to it.' She held my gaze for a moment, before returning to the cellar.

'Sit down,' I said, pulling a chair out for Fazi. There was an awkward silence while I poured tea. 'I didn't think you were coming,' I said, handing him a mug.

'I wanted to get well before you saw me.'

I sat down opposite, cradling the cup in my hands. 'I didn't know what to think. I asked around, but no one's seen you.'

He paused, looking down at the table, then said, 'I was ashamed.' Silence stretched out between us, until he raised his eyes to meet mine. 'I got myself some of your potion though.'

'Are you still taking it?'

He nodded. 'I gave in once, found a leftover stash of Papaver. Your potion really works. The sickness lasted two days. Never again.' He paused then said, 'I know I don't deserve a second chance. But I want you to know I'm proud of you. You take after your mother.'

I stiffened to hear him mention Mata.

'A lot of people are working towards better days,' I said.

'I want to help. I know others do too.'

I sat back in the chair, quietly considering as I held him in my gaze. He didn't look away.

I stood up, paused then said, 'Wait here.'

I went down to the cellar where Zandi was waiting.

'Be careful,' she whispered. 'He's let you down before.'

'I know. But he's come this far, and we could do with all the help we can get.' I paused then added, 'I want to believe I can trust him again.'

She nodded and stood aside, as I went to a sack of bitterweed and pulled out a handful. I paused, glancing at the nearby shelves, smiling at the sight of Mata's old book: a catalogue of herbal lore written in my mother's hand. The last entry was mine: instructions for our potion.

I returned to Fazi and dropped the bitterweed on the table in front of him.

'What's this?' he said.

'Bitterweed, also known as Blue agave. It forms the base of the potion.'

He looked at me, one eyebrow raised in a question.

'It grows in the sacred forest, and we need more of it, much more.'

'You mean…?'

I nodded. 'When the rafts arrive, Zandi and I are leaving for the islands and taking what potion we've got with us. While we're gone, Sisile and Sunette will make more, but they need help collecting the weed.' I paused, seeing hope in his eyes, then said, 'Papaver has ruined too many lives for too long. We're going to start trading in something good for once.'

42. Luna

THE WORLD SAW A TEN-year-old girl touched by a dragon. They saw a hybrid, but they never saw me, the silent part existing between the two extremes. I felt the girl's confusion and the dragon's rage, but my view of the world was clear.

My life had become an endless cycle of repetition, locked into an existence that lived between the forest dream and the tiled room. I was in the tiled room now, the silent part of me standing over the hybrid as she closed her eyes and slowly drifted to sleep. When she opened her eyes, she would be in the forest with no memory of this place. And I would be there by the girl's side. Eventually. But not yet.

The hybrid body was strange and unfamiliar, not like something I belonged to. When I brushed a hand over the skin, thinking to return to the body, nothing happened. The dragon storm had changed me in more ways than people knew. I still felt the dragon's heat like burning cold slicing through my consciousness. Since then I had been unable to return to the body in the waking world or the dream world. I had also come to realise that I was no longer bound to follow the hybrid's consciousness into the dream. But each time she drifted, I followed. I was like a spirit with no home, lost in the world, so I stayed close to what I knew.

I turned to look at Wanda sitting in the chair, sipping a milky concoction that would tip him into sleep. The locket he wore around his neck matched the one worn around the hybrid's. He thought it meant he could save me, but he had yet to save himself. He may have mastered his fear of the shadow bound to him, but he still felt it as a curse.

Wanda's shadow wasn't the only one here: traces of dusty grey still lingered over the hybrid's skin, a reminder of the dragon's embrace. Other shadows appeared from the walls, their cool forms bringing a chill to the air that the silent part of me could feel. I felt at home among the patches of whispering grey.

The latch clicked and the door opened ajar. Eleanor peered in. She reminded me of the woman I had seen in Wanda's shadow, the same woman who had once visited the dream. They both had piercing blue eyes and pale white skin like chalk, although Eleanor's hair was white to match, not red like fire. This was the woman who had stolen Wanda's heart. I gazed longingly as their eyes met and they shared a playful smile. I savoured these times, witnessing the love between them blossom. These were the times I felt closest to life. Eleanor raised her eyebrows in a question but Wanda gently shook his head. He would see her later, but first he would meet the girl in the forest.

Wanda rested his empty mug on the table, then sat back in the chair and closed his eyes. I moved closer to the wall, feeling the cool touch of surrounding shadows creep over my skin. I tilted my head back and closed my eyes, welcoming their embrace as they drew me into their silent world. It was a place of cool mist, like a corridor leading me into the dream. I walked on through to where the air was clear, and stepped out into the forest.

IT WAS A DAY LIKE any other. Birdsong rang throughout the canopy as Wanda and the girl explored familiar pathways. I stayed behind, a mere observer, while Wanda subtly directed the girl, keeping her away from forest clearings where they would be easy prey for the dragon. Under Wanda's watchful eye, the girl inspected animal tracks in the surrounding bush, buds about to flower and eggs about to hatch. I watched, absorbed by her youthful innocence, sad to think how much I missed the feel of the world through her senses.

Every now and again the dragon made its powers known, when the sound of birdsong dipped too low or the leaves on the trees became the wrong shade of green. I looked on, helpless to resist the changes. I was afraid of what it would mean for all of us if the girl was captured. But Wanda was quick to spot the dangers. He had become adept at maintaining the forest as it should be, keeping the girl content in ignorance of the dragon searching for her.

When dusk fell, they set up camp on a bed of spongy aloe grass in the shade of an acatcha tree. Wanda watched over the girl as she closed her eyes. She was unaware that this day would be repeated when the sun rose, or that Wanda was about to leave us alone. Before my eyes he faded from the forest to return to the tiled room, where Eleanor would be waiting.

I stayed behind with the girl, watching her sleep. The night chorus of bats began, the rush as they swarmed up through the trees, and the squeaks of the females and pups in their roosts. Somewhere in the distance came the territorial hoot of an owl, two short, deep 'hoo' sounds followed by a long 'hooooooo'. I listened as the sounds grew gradually higher in pitch, and kept my gaze on the dark silhouette of the girl. The dragon was closing in. I could only hope Wanda would be back by morning, although these days, he was staying away for longer.

First light brought more changes. Moss covering nearby boulders was yellow and dried. Sepia flowers trailing over thick fronds of ground-covering palm were deep indigo instead of the usual pale blue. The girl woke up and saw it too, looking out into the undergrowth, confused. She stood up and called for Wanda, but there was no reply. The morning chorus of birdsong grew quiet, until just a single pine warbler was left singing for its mate in the high bough of a redwood tree. When its pitch dipped too low, the girl set off down the path, desperation growing in her voice as she called Wanda's name.

I followed, helpless to comfort the girl as she searched for Wanda. He had never been gone this long before. She stopped to catch her breath in the middle of a copse of elderbirch. Green lichen covering the trees paled to chalky white, and wisps of smoke came creeping towards us through the undergrowth. The girl wrapped her arms around her waist, looking around with fear in her wide eyes. Leaves rustled as branches stirred in a growing breeze, carrying a whispering voice in the air: '*Oraaag*'. The dragon was closing in, and all I could do was watch and wait for the inevitable.

Out of the corner of my eye I glimpsed colour in the trees that was out of place. I turned and saw the white woman with red hair looking back at me. The last time I had seen her it was just a fleeting glance. This time she came to me. The girl didn't see the woman cup my face in her hands. She had a ghostly form, like me, yet hers was a touch I could feel. She didn't speak, just looked at me with a calm, curious expression. Then she let go of my face and stepped away, holding her arm out and gesturing for me to follow. She led me to a nearby elderbirch tree where she pressed her hand against the bark. When she lifted it away, there was a green handprint in the greyed and discoloured lichen. She closed her fingers around my wrist and raised my arm, gesturing for me to do the same. I hesitated, looking at the chalky lichen, doubting that I had the power to change it back. But the woman pressed my hand down flat against the bark. When I lifted it away, I saw my own green handprint.

This was the power that Wanda had. I raised my hand and pressed it down on another section of bark. This time when I lifted it away, there was no change. I looked at the woman but she just smiled. I wanted to ask how to do it again, but I had no voice. I looked back at my first print, wondering. Wanda knew his ability to alter the dream; he believed in his power to keep the forest as it should be. If I could do it once, I could do it again. I pressed my hand back down, slowly lifted it away and was pleased to see I left a green mark.

The whispering breeze blew stronger. The woman turned and walked away, into the trees where clouds of smoke came spilling down the path. The smoke parted as she walked through, leaving behind a trail of green grass. Feeling danger closing in, I went to the girl, reaching out to her, daring to believe I had the power to save myself. I felt the warmth of her skin, the dry thirst in her mouth, and the pounding of her heart that finally felt like my own. Then the forest turned dark.

I looked around into the trees, now cast in the shadow of the dragon's flight. Beating wings circled overhead, sounding like giant bellows as they pushed gusting air down through the branches. The whispering voice in the air grew louder, sounding like a long low growl: *Oraaag*. With fists clenched and eyes fixed straight ahead, I ran through the trees following the white woman's trail of green.

Spurred on by the sound of beating wings, smoke followed at my heels and ashen grey lichen swept through surrounding trees like a disease. But the pathway of green was leading me away, and slowly I widened the gap. I entered an unfamiliar part of the forest, where ancient trees stood like giants with enormous boughs splayed like open hands. Gaps between the trees grew wider as I closed in on what sounded like the roar of rushing water. I weaved my way through huge boulders littering the path, coming to a sudden stop when the ground gave way to a deep chasm. Perched on a rocky outcrop, I looked out across the bronze cliff faces of a giant gorge, momentarily struck by the dramatic and unexpected landscape hollowed out in the middle of the forest. Edged by trees, across the gorge a waterfall dropped down to blue waters that filled the basin. I peered down at the clouds of foaming spray, absorbed by the resounding cascade.

I stepped back from the edge and started down a path, intending to make my way to the other side of the gorge. Seeing tendrils of smoke sweeping across the ground towards me, I backed away, turning to head in the opposite direction. But all around me, smoke was creeping over boulders and through undergrowth. I looked out into the trees where ashen lichen smothered the branches, hoping the white woman might return to me. But there was no sign of her. Pinned to the edge of the cliff, the roaring waterfall was all I could hear. But seeing treetops sway in the gusting air, I imagined the sound of beating wings encroaching.

A sudden shriek rang out in the sky, deafening all else, before the dragon appeared over the trees. Its arched leathery wings appeared translucent, revealing the pattern of veins against a bright blue sky. It hovered overhead, balanced by a sweeping, horned tail. I felt the burning cold in my belly as I looked up at the dragon's huge talons. When fire came gushing from its open jaws, I edged back, feeling loose stone fall away beneath my heels.

I closed my eyes, leaned back, and fell.

43. Luna

WINDED BY A SUDDEN CRASH landing, I opened my eyes to find myself sprawled on the dragon's broad back, scooped up out of my fall. The cliffs towered above as the beast twisted and turned, screeching as it struggled to lift its massive bulk from the descent. The barbed tail swung from side to side as it fought to steady itself out of the coiling flight. I scrambled up onto my knees and reached for two bony ridges to anchor myself between the beating wings, as the dragon's angular head reached up, jaws open, shrieking in fury.

Time seemed to slow into one unmoving frame, as I considered a future consumed by the beast. I pushed forward and tried to stand, thinking to jump. A fire breathing dragon would surely not follow into water. But my hands and knees were strangely numb. I looked down in horror to see grey scales creeping up my fingers, blending with the dragon's leathery skin. A strange, inky black substance was oozing out from beneath my hands. I managed to prize one hand free but threads of black goo clung to my skin, binding me to the pool of black bubbling up out of the dragon's hide. I looked down at my knees that were also embedded in black pools, and saw the same grey scales spreading, turning my legs mottled grey. Weighted down by the binding black, I imagined the warm sticky substance seeping into my flesh.

Feeling a sudden painful pounding in my chest, I gasped, forced to lean forwards. The pain quickly subsided, and I was left with the realisation that I could feel two hearts pounding in my chest. The burning cold in my belly turned to searing heat that caught in the back

167

of my throat, hot like fire. I screwed my eyes shut and gritted my teeth, refusing to succumb. But behind closed eyes I saw myself kneeling on the ground, surrounded by a circle of flames. Leaning forward with my back arched, the skin of my shoulder blades split as leathery wings sprouted.

A sudden spray of water jolted me from my vision. The fire in my belly momentarily cooled as I looked at my leg where the spray had hit, seeing patches of unnatural grey scales where the smearing black had been washed away. Two hearts still pounded in my chest, but this time I didn't turn from the dragon's power. I kicked my foot and dug my knee hard into the hide of the dragon's left side. Black ooze bubbled up and over my arms and legs, as I felt myself slowly sinking into the dragon's flesh. I yelled out, pushing forwards then leaning my upper body out to the side. The dragon responded, veering sharply left, closer to the waterfall. Its cries filled the skies when clouds of spray hit, washing away the goo that bound me to the beast. I lifted myself up to stand, turned and jumped.

The sudden cascade of water hit with a force so hard it took my breath away. I spun, twisting and jarring before being slammed against cold stone. I looked out, dazed, from behind the waterfall, sprawled on a broad ledge jutting out from the cliffside. Above the roaring falls, the dragon's cries sounded distant, but I could see its hovering silhouette through the curtain of water. I pulled myself up, rubbed my grazed arms and bloodied knees. It was a relief to see my skin had returned to normal. I looked around to get my bearings, hoping for a way out, and saw a narrow opening in the rock. I peered in and found it opened out into a cave.

It was a deep cavern with branching tunnels burrowing into the cliff. I ventured in and down a tunnel high enough for me to walk upright, wondering whether it might lead to daylight and an escape from the dragon. When the tunnel divided, I veered left but came to a dead end. I turned back to retrace my steps. It happened again and again until I was disorientated. I stopped, leaning back against the damp wall, rubbing my sore arms as the air turned cool. In the dim light I watched a strange grey haze creep along the ground towards me. At first I wondered if it was the dragon's powers of illusion, but it wasn't thick like smoke, more like an early morning mist. I went towards it, feeling it cool against my ankles as I walked in the direction it was coming from, hoping it might lead to the outside. It grew deeper, swirling up over my legs, up to my waist then shoulders, until it filled the tunnel and I couldn't see. I stopped, reaching back, fumbling for the wall but my hands felt only cool air. I looked out blindly, afraid I had walked straight into the dragon's trap.

Faint voices filled the air: whispering, laughing, crying, coming from all directions. Cooler than the air, a deep chill brushed against the back of my neck. I turned and glimpsed the figure of a man before he disappeared into the mist. A moment later, a woman and child walked by, close enough for me to see the ashen skin of their ghostly forms. Other ghosts came and went, oblivious to my presence as they brushed against me. A woman appeared, walking straight towards me with an orb of light held in her cupped hands. Unlike the others, her skin was warm and alive. She stopped in front of me, held the light up to my face, and smiled as though she had been expecting me.

'Luna?' she said.

I raised my eyebrows in surprise. 'Who are you?'

'A friend. My name is Mata.'

I looked closer, seeing something familiar in her eyes.

'What is this place?' I asked. 'Am I still dreaming?'

'No. You left the dream.'

'How?'

'The how is not important. Only the why.'

I gazed into her eyes, searching. 'How do you know me?'

'Because you know my daughter, Suni. You are Wanda's cousin.'

Now I remembered where I'd heard the name before.

'Then you're... dead,' I whispered.

'Some might say that.'

Fixed in her gaze, I wrapped my arms around my waist and asked, 'What is this place? Where am I?'

'You found your way into *Serafay*, the corridor between dreams. Only the dead or a dreamwalker can know this place, or, in your case, a mage?'

169

I looked at her, curious, and asked, 'Do you know about the dragon?'

'I know enough,' she said. 'I know you have been frightened and alone, trapped by a power that is consuming you. And I know you found a way to escape.'

'I got away from the dragon, but now I am nowhere.'

She smiled and said, 'It is true, the corridors are a maze for those without a destination. But if you come with me, I can take you to a place where you will never again have to be afraid.'

I hesitated, then murmured, 'You mean die.'

'Death is just a beginning.'

She turned to the side and held out the orb of light. I watched its radiating glow light a window in the mist. Colours began to form in the grey haze, faint at first but growing bolder and brighter, until a world of trees appeared before me.

'It's the forest,' I said, confused, as I looked back at Mata.

'It's not the forest you know,' she said. 'This is the Land Beyond, a hidden place that you could call home. It's a forest where there are no dragons.'

44. Suni

ONCE AGAIN, THE RAFTS PROVIDED passage to the islands. For Juna and Ntombi it was the first time they had left the mainland, yet they said little on the voyage. Ever since Luna's transformation, they had been lost on an island of grief. I was glad they had each other, and hoped that visiting might bring some comfort.

Arriving at the docks of Evren, Nisrin and others from the rafts set about handing out potion and tending to the sick. We left them there, Zandi and I leading us on up the main street, as Juna wheeled Ntombi in her chair. At the temple gates we received Reynauld's sombre greeting, before he quietly led us to where Eleanor was waiting in the entrance. There was vulnerability in the priestess's tired eyes, weak smile and slumped posture.

'I'm glad you're here,' she said.

'What is it?' I asked. 'What's wrong?'

She glanced at each of us in turn then said, 'Follow me. I'll take you to Luna's room.'

She led the way into the entrance hall, where Sylvie, the apprentice, was busy smoothing mortar between the tiles. Despite her efforts, mist was seeping through.

'What is that?' Zandi asked, looking straight at the drifting mist.

Eleanor looked back and said, 'Come, please. There's not much time.'

She led the way down a branching hallway, arriving at the door to Luna's room.

Inside the tiled room, Luna lay curled on the bed, facing the wall where tiles were replaced with a scaled, leathery surface mottled in shades of grey. I stood back with Zandi, while Ntombi stood up and went to her daughter's bedside, closely followed by Juna. They huddled together, leaning over Luna.

Moments later, Ntombi turned back to Eleanor, a look of surprise on her face as she said, 'I don't know how to thank you.'

'Don't thank me,' Eleanor said. 'Luna won't wake up. I don't know how this happened.'

I went to the bed and saw Luna appearing like her like her old self, with no sign of hybrid features. I turned back to Eleanor, but she had moved to the far corner where an old man was sleeping in an armchair. I had assumed he was one of the old warders, but when she held a lantern closer, I saw his complexion was dark. He stirred when she rested a hand on his shoulder, recognition slowly spreading across his face as his watery gaze rested on me.

'Suni.' Despite the huskiness, it was Wanda's voice.

'It can't be,' I whispered.

'It's true,' Eleanor said. 'We don't know why, but as Luna lost her hybrid features, Wanda aged.'

I heard Ntombi's sharp cry and Juna utter, 'This isn't making any sense.' But I was too stunned to speak. With eyes fixed on Wanda I walked slowly towards him, knelt down and reached for his hand, feeling the softs folds of his sagging skin.

'I lost Luna,' he said. 'It's been over a week since I last saw her in the dream.'

'We've never known this happen before,' Eleanor said. 'We think Luna must have somehow wandered into *Serafay*.'

'But how?' I said, looking up at Eleanor. 'How is any of this possible?'

'It must be because Luna is *Maravin*,' Eleanor said. 'We couldn't be sure what that would mean, but somehow, she has found a way to leave the dream.' She pulled the shawl tight around her shoulders. 'If we can't bring her back, she will die, and Wanda will die with her.'

'*Serafay* is the corridor between dreams,' I said. 'It isn't death.'

'But Luna's mind is lost there,' Eleanor said. 'The body can't live long without the mind. Wanda shares her fate since they are connected by the warder's bond.'

'There must be something we can do,' Ntombi cried.

I looked back at Wanda, gently squeezing his hand.

'Did something happen in the dream?' I asked. 'Maybe if you try again.'

He held me in his watery gaze. 'I searched for her. She was gone before fires came and the forest burned.'

IT WAS THE EARLY HOURS of morning before we finally went to bed, but I couldn't sleep. I sat on the edge of the bed listening to Zandi softly snore, as I gazed into the warm glow of candlelight burning on the bedside table. Restless, I draped a shawl over my shoulders, reached for the lantern and went over to the tiled wall. Holding the light up to tendrils of mist drifting over the mosaic, I dipped my fingers into the cool haze. *Luna, where are you?*

'Suni.'

Startled by the whispering voice, I quickly turned and held up the lantern. When I saw my mother looking back at me, I dropped my arm and stumbled back into the wall. For a moment I just stared into the dark, before I slowly raised the lantern again. Shocked into silence, I gazed into Mata's eyes, barely daring to blink in case she disappeared. Her spirit had visited me before, but this was the first time since her death. Now, caught in the scent of her soul, I was cast back to all the aromas of home.

Finally, I whispered, 'Why now?'

She smiled and said, 'A part of me has always been with you, seeing the world through your eyes.'

I felt the cool of her touch as she reached out, tracing her finger alongside the tear rolling down my cheek. In that moment I imagined Mata existing in every part of my being, in the very air I breathed, in the tears I cried, in every thought and word that had ever passed between my lips.

'I've come to help you, Suni. Luna is with me in *Serafay.*'

'How?' I uttered.

'There is more to Luna than you realise,' she said. 'Luna knows about the dragon and what Wanda is trying to do. She knows all of it, and she escaped. She left the dream, but she can't stay in *Serafay*.'

'How do I bring her back?' I asked.

'You don't.' She paused then said, 'She wants to be free. You have to let her go.'

'You mean die?' I shook my head. 'There must be another way.'

'The girl and the dragon are one and the same. You cannot separate Luna from herself, and Luna is no longer willing to live alongside the dragon.'

I thought of the baby I had held in my arms, scarred from the fire in the mountains. The fire had cursed her young life and Luna had grown into a complex, distant girl that I had never really understood. Yet perhaps all this time she had known what the rest of us did not.

'Her family will never let her go,' I said.

'Then you must make them understand. Luna cannot just exist for their sakes. She can come with me and find her place in the forests of the Land Beyond.'

I quietly gazed into my mother's eyes, reminded of the woman she had been in life: reasoned in her thinking, determined in her search for truth, with little time for sentiment.

Seeing her slowly drift away from me, I stepped forward and said, 'But what about Wanda?'

'Bring him to the cellars, to the origin of Serafay. I will be waiting with Luna.' She was disappearing into the misty wall. 'It's not Wanda's time. If the warder's bond is broken before Luna leaves, he will survive.'

'Don't go,' I whispered to myself.

But she was gone.

'Your mother is a soul seeker.' I turned to see Eleanor standing in the doorway. 'She offers lost souls a path to peace.' There was hope in her eyes as she walked towards me. 'By the grace of the temple, the cellars haven't been opened for centuries. The origin is one room and a maze of many.' She slipped her hand in mine and gently squeezed. 'But you are a dreamwalker, like your mother. There is a chance you might find each other.'

'But I don't know what she meant,' I said, 'about breaking the warder's bond.'

She fingered the locket at her throat. 'I can help you there.'

45. Suni

APPROACHING THE DOOR TO LUNA'S room, I shuddered inside. How to tell parents they must say goodbye to their child? Yet they must. Nothing could be done to reverse Luna's fate, but every moment we delayed took us closer to Wanda's life meeting an unnecessary end. My stomach turned as I pushed the door open and went inside.

Ntombi and Juna were already resigned to their loss. They had seen enough to know we could not fight against the powers holding Luna hostage. Their faces were tear-stained but their tears had run dry. The glimmer of hope they had been given had turned out to be nothing more than a cruel twist of fate. It was small comfort, but I was glad they were at least able to say goodbye to Luna's human form.

They stayed by their daughter's side, holding vigil, while Eleanor and I helped Wanda into Ntombi's chair. As we wheeled him out and down through the hallways, I listened to Wanda's laboured breathing, fearing he was running out of time. All the changes affecting our lives seemed to alter the temple too. The layers of tiles built up over the years, the carefully maintained mortar, could no longer keep *Serafay* at bay. All around the walls, floor and ceiling, mist was oozing through the cracks.

Eleanor led the way into an unused section of the temple, where mist covering the floor was ankle deep. Zandi was there with Reynauld, taking turns with a mallet to smash through layers of tiles on the ground. They uncovered a wooden hatch that laid entrance to the cellars, a sealed doorway that had remained hidden for centuries. When the hatch was prized open, clouds of *Serafay* poured out into the passageway, filling the air with whispering voices carried in the haze.

Eleanor handed me a lantern and said, 'It's up to you to lead the way, Suni.'

I glanced nervously down the hatch, through the swirling mist, catching sight of steep steps leading below ground. I had never navigated *Serafay* when I was awake, and was sure my hidden sense would be no use in searching for my mother's spirit. I could only hope Mata would find me, but, looking at Wanda's frail body, I needed more than hope.

Zandi came to stand beside me, put a hand on my shoulder and gently squeezed.

'You'll find a way,' she said. 'You always do.'

Held in her gaze, I slowly nodded, before reaching down with one foot then the next.

Eleanor followed, slowly manoeuvring Wanda in the chair, as I led the way down into the cellar. When we reached solid ground, I linked an arm through hers, holding the lantern up with my other hand as I guided us forwards. Like navigating the corridors between dreams, ghostly figures crossed our path, but I saw nothing familiar among the mournful faces. I stared into the mist waiting for a sign, but there was no hint of a breeze in the still air. I kept going, not knowing what to expect but telling myself, somehow, my mother would find a way to reach me. Hearing running footsteps, I paused. I had never heard such a clear sound in *Serafay* before.

'Don't get distracted,' Eleanor whispered. 'We have to keep moving.'

The deeper we went, more sounds came: a child's cry, the sound of laughter then tears. My thoughts were confused, wondering whether I was listening to the dead, or dreamers. Until my mother's voice, calling my name, broke through the confusion. I turned in the direction of her voice, and saw a faint light flickering in the grey haze. I led the way, walking towards it, and saw Mata appear in the mist, holding the light in her cupped hands. She smiled as her eyes met mine, then looked down to the side, as Luna stepped out from behind her.

Where Mata's apparition appeared in ghostly tones of grey, Luna's spirit form possessed all the colours of the living. There were no signs of the dragon, no hybrid features, not even the scar from being burned as a baby marked her cheek. When her gaze met mine, there was a discerning look in her eyes, revealing a side of Luna I didn't recognise. I thought back to what Mata had said, wondering just how much Luna had kept from her family, from all of us. Alone, a ten-year-old girl had faced the horrors that had long cast a shadow over my homeland. She had been blamed, feared and misunderstood, and yet all along she had known the truth about the dragon.

The calm expression on Luna's face turned to confusion then fright as her eyes rested on Wanda, recognition flashing across her face.

'Don't be afraid,' Wanda said, inching forward in his chair.

'But how? What happened to you?' she asked.

Mata put a hand on Luna's shoulder. 'Wanda is bonded to you, Luna, and we've stayed here too long.'

Luna stepped closer to her cousin. 'You're like this because I came here?'

'We're both like this because of the dragon,' Wanda said. He paused then added, 'I should never have left you. I should never have stayed away so long. Turn back and return to the dream. We can go back to the way things were. I can keep you safe.'

Luna shook her head. 'I don't want to go back to the way things were.' She paused, eyes narrowing in a thoughtful gaze. 'I know more than you think and I'm not afraid. I can look after myself.' She paused then said, 'Besides, you've got a new life now.'

Wanda held Luna in a silent gaze, as though seeing her for the first time.

Finally, he said, 'I always thought you needed me, but perhaps it was the other way around.' He paused, eyes shining. '*You* faced a dragon and escaped. You must be the bravest person I know.'

She smiled. 'Mata's taking me to the Land Beyond.'

Wanda slowly nodded and wiped away a tear. 'I went there once. I think you'll like it. It's like the forests of home.'

'No, not like home,' Luna said. 'Mata says there are no dragons in the forests of the Land Beyond.'

Watching their goodbyes, I saw more love between them than I had known existed. The closeness of kin had been literally bonded, and now, the very thing that tied them together was forcing them to part.

'It's time,' Mata said.

Eleanor undid the locket from around Wanda's neck and held it in the palm of her hand. Mata did the same with Luna's. Like Luna, her locket had no physical form, until it was dropped into Eleanor's hand, sounding with a quiet tap as the two knocked together. Then Eleanor pressed her hands together, holding the lockets inside as she raised her clasped hands to her lips and closed her eyes.

'*Tukama saransha divinda*,' she whispered over and over. '*Tukama saransha divinda.*'

The spell carried in the gentle breeze that stirred, circling around Luna and Wanda. Wanda slowly transformed back to his youthful self: his sagging skin filled out, his posture straightened, and his hair thickened and returned to brown. But for Luna, the rich brown of her skin was fading to grey.

'Look,' Mata said.

Beside her, weaves in the mist unravelled, revealing a window into another world. I recognised the forest landscape with its winding river and pathway into the trees. The last time I had seen the Land Beyond, it had appeared to me in tones of grey. This time I saw the colours of nature revealed.

Seeing two people walking arm in arm along the path, I leaned in closer and whispered, 'It can't be.' It was Gogo and Faru, the man I had once looked upon as a father.

Wanda slipped his hand in mine, his eyes shining with tears as Luna stepped one foot into the window.

She paused, looking back at him, and said, 'Maybe I'll see you in the forest someday.'

Their gaze lingered, a warm smile spreading across Luna's face before she turned and walked through the window. She diminished before our eyes, while in the Land Beyond, a breeze stirred through the trees.

Moments later, Luna reappeared on the forest pathway, where Gogo and Faru were waiting.

'Someone else is here,' Mata said, gesturing to the side where a man appeared in the mist.

'Father?' Eleanor said.

Like Luna, his spirit form was free of hybrid features. Seeing his human face, the family resemblance was clear in the soft curve of his rounded jaw and deep-set eyes.

Eleanor raised a hand to her mouth, tears in her eyes as she said, 'I had no idea. What are you doing here?'

He smiled and said, 'I've been here many times before, just to feel some relief from the beast. But I always came back to you.' His gaze drifted to the forest window. 'But now there is another way. Knowing that you will see me as a man before I leave, is more than I could have hoped for.'

'I would have watched over you until the end of my days,' Eleanor said.

Her father shook his head. 'It's time we were both free.'

46. Wanda

I GRIEVED FOR THE LIFE Luna had been denied, and the future that would never be hers. Since losing her, I felt a part of me was missing. Quite simply, I missed my cousin. I was a warder with no one to ward for, with no role to give meaning and purpose to my days. And so I focused on the mundane, taking some comfort in routine.

Sweat channelled down my spine as I stoked the fires of the beacon. Much had changed, but the storm over the Dragon Lands still raged. With the fire blazing, I turned to look out over the seascape. Watching a flock of gulls fly overhead, hearing their noisy chatter as they returned to their nests in the cliffs, I felt a pang of longing. I could reach out with my mind, spread my wings in the salty air and fly. But since the eagle, I had promised myself never to see the world through eyes except my own, and I had kept that promise. Wildlife had once been my refuge, but those days felt like a lifetime ago. As the shadow brushed past my back, I recalled the day the Mantra had turned its back on me.

'I thought I'd find you here.'

I turned to see Eleanor appear from the stairwell. She came and rested her head on my shoulder as we looked out to sea. I smiled, warmed by her presence, and kissed the top of her head. Since her father had left, without anyone to ward for, her hair had darkened to brown. I smoothed my fingers over her braids, rested my hand on her shoulder, and contemplated how life had moved on.

Two more hybrids had been released from their fate, their human bodies laid to rest alongside Eleanor's father in the grounds of the temple. Afterwards, the temple walls had been resealed, once again confining *Serafay* to the cellars. I raised my other hand to my neck, brushing my fingers against my throat where the locket had once been. It was a month since I had gifted it to Ntombi, as something to remember Luna by. Afterwards they had left with the rafts, taking Luna's body home to Shendi.

'I've been thinking,' Eleanor said.

'Oh?'

She wrapped an arm around my waist and gently squeezed. 'I've been thinking maybe we should leave.'

I turned to face her. 'And go where?'

'To your homeland.' She reached up, cupping my cheek in her hand. 'You don't belong here now Luna's gone.'

'I belong with you.'

'That's true.' She kissed me on the lips, then said. 'I see how your people look at you. I see what they see: a boy from a valley filled with wildlife and trees.' She paused then said, 'Don't you miss it? Don't you miss home?'

Moments passed and I held her gaze. I did miss it. But I was afraid. I glanced at the shadow lurking close by.

'I'm stronger here,' I said, looking back at Eleanor.

She shook her head. 'The shadow has no power over you unless you let it. You've learnt that for yourself. All you've learned, the strength you've found in your time here, will stay with you beyond this place.'

'Maybe that's true. But this is *your* home.'

'Not anymore. Now that my father's gone, I'm not needed here.'

'But the dragons are still here,' I said.

'Yes, and by the grace of the temple the warders will continue their work. But they don't need me.' She looked away, gazing out across the seascape. 'I've spent so much of my life in the dream world. It was the only other place I saw until I travelled to Shendi. I want more from my life. I want to see more, know more.' She turned back to face me. 'You and your family are my family now.'

I DIDN'T THINK I WOULD see Shendi again, but I returned to the valley with Eleanor by my side. At her request, we built our cottage close to Juna and Ntombi's. By night we were visited by howling wolves, by day we watched herds of passing deer. But while Eleanor explored the grasslands, I stayed close to home tending crops, always with the shadow close by like a stray with no home.

Sweat soaked through my shirt as I dug over new ground ready for planting. I looked up as Eleanor approached, smiling to see her waddling walk, her stomach swollen with our coming child.

'I'll get you a chair,' I said, planting the spade in the ground.

'I'm fine,' she said. 'Stop fussing.' She held her cupped hands out to me, carefully revealing a young sparrow. 'It must have fallen from the nest.' When I made no move she added, 'Juna told me about all the creatures you used to nurse back to health.'

'That was a long time ago,' I said, pulling the spade up.

'Don't turn your back on the best parts of you.'

Stilled by her words, I stopped and looked at the fuzzy chick. Without help, it would be dead in a few days. Still I hesitated.

'I know what's on your mind. I know what you're afraid of.' She tipped the sparrow into one hand, and reached for my hand with the other, placing it to rest on her stomach. I sighed to feel the baby kick, rubbing a gentle hand over the bulging bump. 'You lost Luna, but you won't lose this baby. Our daughter will soon be here, and I want you to teach her all the things you were taught as a boy.'

Tears pricked my eyes as I met Eleanor's gaze. She always saw the truths I tried to hide. Now it was fear I wouldn't be able to protect our child, like I hadn't saved Luna. I leaned forward and kissed her, then reached for the chick, feeling life in its pulsing heartbeat as I held it in my cupped hands.

'Now come,' she said. 'I saw Suni and Zandi arriving.'

Eleanor picked a bunch of purple violets on the way to Juna and Ntombi's cottage. Suni came out to meet us as we approached.

'Another rescue,' she said with a smile, looking at the sparrow.

Eleanor kissed her on the cheek. 'It's been so long since we've seen you.'

'I know,' Suni said. 'We've been busy teaching the townsfolk herbal lore.' She raised her eyebrows. 'Those are words I never thought I'd say.'

'Any sign of the poaching trade?' I asked.

'No, thankfully. Things are finally changing. And now, with the blight gone, there are no more chicken feet hanging on the doors.' When I frowned, she laughed. 'There's a new saying in town: misfortune seeks misfortune. I hardly recognise the place.' She linked her arm through mine and Eleanor's. 'Come, the others are with Luna.'

We went around the back of the cottage, where Juna, Ntombi and Zandi were waiting. Gathered beside a young acatcha tree standing guard over Luna's grave, we huddled together in quiet contemplation of the anniversary of her death. Eleanor knelt down laying violets on the mound. I helped her back up and reached for Ntombi's hand, resting it on Eleanor's bump.

'We will call her Luna-Mae.'

Other novels, novellas and short story collections available from Stairwell Books. Scifi and Climate Change themed books are highlighted.

Life Lessons by Libby	Libby and Laura Engel-Sahr
Waters of Time	Pauline Kirk
Waiting at the Temporary Traffic Lights	Graham Lee
The Tao of Revolution	**Chris Taylor**
The Water Bailiff's Daughter	Yvonne Hendrie
O Man of Clay	**Eliza Mood**
Eboracvm: the Village	Graham Clews
Sammy Blue Eyes	Frank Beill
Margaret Clitherow	John and Wendy Rayne-Davis
Serpent Child	Pat Riley
Rocket Boy	John Wheatcroft
Virginia	Alan Smith
Connecting North	Thelma Laycock
Looking for Githa	Patricia Riley
On Suicide Bridge	Tom Dixon
Something I Need to Tell You	William Thirsk-Gaskill
Poetic Justice	P J Quinn
Return of the Mantra	**Susie Williamson**
The Martyrdoms at Clifford's Tower 1190 and 1537	John Rayne-Davis
The Go-To Guy	Neal Hardin
Abernathy	Claire Patel-Campbell
Tyrants Rex	**Clint Wastling**
A Shadow in My Life	Rita Jerram
Rapeseed	Alwyn Marriage
Thinking of You Always	Lewis Hill
Know Thyself	Lance Clarke
How to be a Man	Alan Smith
Here in the Cull Valley	John Wheatcroft
Tales from a Prairie Journal	Rita Jerram
Border 7	**Pauline Kirk**
Homelands	Shaunna Harper
49	Paul Lingaard
The Geology of Desire	Clint Wastling
When the Crow Cries	**Maxine Ridge**
Close Disharmony	P J Quinn
Wine Dark, Sea Blue	A.L. Michael
Poison Pen	P J Quinn
Foul Play	PJ Quinn
A Day at the Races	N.E. David
Feria	N.E. David

For further information please contact rose@stairwellbooks.com

www.stairwellbooks.co.uk
@stairwellbooks

Lightning Source UK Ltd.
Milton Keynes UK
UKHW010012130321
380247UK00001B/51